The Rebel

Nancy Rue

PUBLISHING
Colorado Springs, Colorado

THE REBEL
Copyright © 1996 by Nancy N. Rue
All rights reserved. International copyright secured.

Library of Congress Cataloging-in-Publication Data
Rue, Nancy N.
    The rebel / Nancy Rue.
        p.   cm.— (Christian heritage series ; bk. 7)
    Summary: Ten-year-old Thomas Hutchinson struggles with his rebellious nature in the
face of a stern father while also experiencing the rising tensions caused by the
Revolutionary War.
    ISBN 1-56179-478-3
    [1. Fathers and sons—Fiction. 2. United States—History—Revolution, 1775-1783—
Fiction. 3. Christian life—Fiction.] I. Title. II. Series: Rue, Nancy N. Christian heritage
series ; bk. 7.
PZ7.R88515Rad   1996
[Fic]—dc20   96-8549
                                                                              CIP
                                                                              AC

Published by Focus on the Family Publishing,
Colorado Springs, Colorado 80995
Distributed in the U.S.A. and Canada by Word Books, Dallas, Texas.

This author is represented by the literary agency of Alive Communications, 1465 Kelly
Johnson Blvd., Suite 320, Colorado Springs, CO 80920.

This is a work of fiction, and any resemblance between the characters in this book and real
persons is coincidental.

Focus on the Family books are available at special quantity discounts when purchased in
bulk by corporations, organizations, churches, or groups. Special imprints, messages, and
excerpts can be produced to meet your needs. For more information, write: Special Sales
Department, Focus on the Family Publishing, 8605 Explorer Drive, Colorado Springs, CO
80920, or call (719) 531-3400 and ask for the Special Sales Department.

Editor: Keith Wall
Cover Design: Bradley Lind
Cover Illustration: Cheri Bladholm

Printed in the United States of America

96 97 98 99 00/10 9 8 7 6 5 4 3 2 1

For Carly, Andrew, Kalyn, Bradley,
Michael, Steven, Madeline, and Kayla . . .
The new generation of rebels!

A Map of
Williamsburg
1780–81

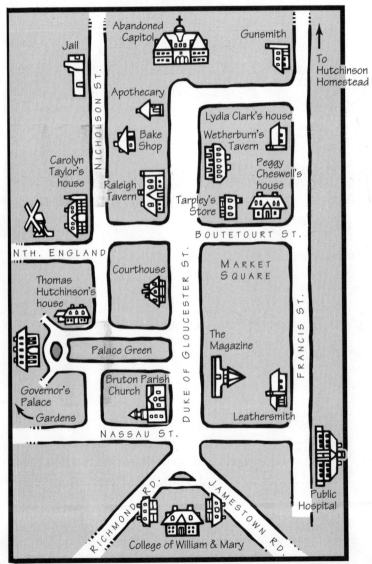

Jail

Abandoned Capitol

Gunsmith

To Hutchinson Homestead

NICHOLSON ST.

Apothecary

Lydia Clark's house

Bake Shop

Wetherburn's Tavern

Carolyn Taylor's house

Raleigh Tavern

Peggy Cheswell's house

Tarpley's Store

BOUTETOURT ST.

NTH. ENGLAND

Courthouse

MARKET SQUARE

Thomas Hutchinson's house

DUKE OF GLOUCESTER ST.

FRANCIS ST.

Palace Green

The Magazine

Governor's Palace

Bruton Parish Church

Gardens

Leathersmith

NASSAU ST.

Public Hospital

RICHMOND RD.

JAMESTOWN RD.

College of William & Mary

Chapter One

"Thomas Hutchinson! Let go of that boy at once!"

Thomas Hutchinson darted his deep-set blue eyes up at his older brother and set his square young jaw. But he didn't loosen his grip on the arm of the boy whose freckles stood out like frightened specks on his face.

"Unhand him, I say!" Clayton Hutchinson wrapped his own fingers around Thomas's arm and wrenched it away, lace ruffles flying at his sleeves as he pulled.

"I heard you." Thomas rubbed sulkily at his arm and pouted at the freckle-nosed boy who had retreated to a corner of the schoolroom in tears. "I didn't hurt him. He's nothing but a sissy."

"You hush now!" Clayton sighed wearily and waved his lacy-cuffed hand, first at the circle of servant children at the table who were gazing, open-mouthed, from their hornbooks, and then at the freckled boy. "Run on to the kitchen now, Patrick—all of you. We've finished with lessons for today."

The children snatched up their hornbooks and their New England Primers and fled. Patrick gave one last withered look at Thomas before he skittered from the room.

Thomas flopped into the red chair by the window and watched Clayton catch his breath and limp toward him.

1

Clayton had a weak heart and a shriveled leg, but Thomas had noticed that that didn't keep his brother from pacing up and down and delivering long-winded lectures to him.

Here it comes, he thought. *Another long speech about being a gentleman—because I'm going to become a Virginia planter someday and must know how to treat the servants— blah, blah, blah—take an interest in natural history and mechanics and know the law—blah, blah, blah.* Thomas sniffed loudly. If the high and mighty Clayton had a lowly servant calling *him* "clumsy" and "stumblejohn" while the schoolmaster wasn't looking, *he'd* surely try to wrestle the fellow to the ground, too.

Besides, Thomas thought, as far as he could see, being a Virginia country gentleman meant riding in a coach pulled by six horses, and eating off silver engraved with his family's coat of arms.

"Don't start sniveling, young man," Clayton said.

So Thomas shrugged and bore his eyes into the square toes of his brother's black shoes, which were now planted in front of his chair. The sun that filtered in through the crack between the heavy drapes behind him glinted off the silver buckles and made him squint.

"Sit up, Thomas!" Clayton barked. "And stop screwing up your eyes. Come on, then, face me like a man!"

Stubbornly, Thomas let his eyes crawl up the white stockings, but only as far as the shiny buttons at the knees of Clayton's britches. Clay gave the expected weary sigh.

"What am I to do with you, Thomas?" Clayton said wearily. "Ever since I took on the job as teacher, you've been nothing but trouble. You refuse to study. You gaze out the window during lessons as if you expect to see frogs flying past. You frighten the other students until they cower the minute you walk in the door. I don't have one-tenth the trouble with all seven of those young servants as I do with you, my own brother."

Thomas rolled his eyes. He'd heard this so many times, he could almost say it himself, word for word.

You are a Hutchinson, young man. That means something here in Virginia. Your great-great-grandfather did not bring his family here all the way from Massachusetts in 1692 and build this plantation and make a name for this family to have you blacken it now in 1780 with your laziness and your stubbornness. And furthermore, a gentleman never uses his fists unless he has to protect his honor, and at this point, Thomas, you have *no honor—although well you should, being 10 years old, almost 11—and with a war for independence going on in the northern colonies. You should be doing your best to help in these troubled times. Instead, you're becoming* more *of a burden. You're lucky Papa's not around to see it. I suggest you turn yourself about before he returns from Richmond.*

But Thomas suddenly bolted upright in the red chair and stared at his brother. Had Clayton said, "It's too late to turn yourself about now, Thomas. Papa's on his way back from Richmond this minute"?

The triumphant shine in Clayton's smooth, gray eyes and the thin smile set calmly on his face told Thomas he had.

"Papa?" Thomas asked. "Papa's coming home today?"

"That he is," Clayton said smugly. "And I see I've finally found something that strikes fear in your heart."

Thomas flung himself from the chair and squared his jaw up at Clayton, who even at 19 was only a head and a half taller than he was. "You're a liar, Clayton Hutchinson," he said.

"Call me what you will, but why else would Sam have

ridden out from the college except to greet Papa?"

"Sam? Sam is coming, too?"

Clay folded his arms smartly across his chest. "You must try to be more aware of your surroundings, Thomas," he said. "Sam is already here."

Thomas tore for the window, catching his toe on the leg of the chair and stumbling into the window seat. He thrust aside the heavy drapes and plastered his face and hands against the glass. The terrace that stepped down gracefully from the front of the Hutchinsons' plantation mansion to the gardens below was empty except for the servants patiently hoeing.

"I don't see Sam anywhere," Thomas said.

"That could be because you have no eyes in the back of your head!" a voice sang out.

Thomas twisted around with a jerk and pitched headfirst off the window seat. His brother Sam sent up the shout that always came before his tumbling laughter. He pulled Thomas to his feet.

"You've not changed much, little brother!" he said, his tiny blue eyes dancing. "Still toppling over your own toes!"

Thomas grinned and shrugged and shuffled the toes in question. He hated to be clumsy in front of his 16-year-old brother, but Sam was the only one who could tell him he was an oaf without raising Thomas's hackles. Thomas wanted to be just like him.

"What are you doing here?" Thomas asked. "Why aren't you in school?"

Sam gave that sure grin that made him look as if he knew everything. "I wish I could tell you that the College of William and Mary finally had the good sense to shut down and send us all off to win the war." Sam let some laughter tumble down. "I'm here to meet Papa when he comes home today."

Over Sam's shoulder, Thomas could see Clayton's pale eyebrows twitching with an I-told-you-so. Thomas felt the hair standing up on the back of his neck.

"Why did everyone know except me?" he said.

"What would you have done if you had known?" Sam asked merrily. "Brushed your hair, I hope."

Thomas slapped at the wisps of dark hair that insisted on poking out from the tail he tied with a ribbon at his neck. Esther, one of his father's servants, had always said his hair was as stubborn as he was.

Sam turned to Clayton. "I hope Papa has news of the war. They tell us almost nothing at the college, and now that Thomas Jefferson has moved the capitol from Williamsburg to Richmond—"

"You'll be hard put to find anything out from Papa," Clayton said. "He hates the war."

"He hates the fighting and the bloodshed," Sam said. "But he supports the cause. He wants the colonies to be independent from England." Thomas watched as Sam's face darkened into a scowl. "We had no choice but to go to war against the British and their American Loyalists."

"I'd like to see you try to convince Papa of that," Clay said. "John Hutchinson is a stubborn man."

"But he's no Loyalist!" Sam cried. "He's a Patriot through and through—just as I am!"

Thomas sidled closer to Sam and tossed his head back. "What are *you*, Clayton?"

Clayton narrowed his eyes at Thomas. "I'm a man of God."

"You may not have a church to preach in when we colonists win the war," Sam said. "What American will want to go to the Church of *England?*"

"The Church will live on . . . as long as I am a minister."

"You aren't even ordained yet!" Thomas said. He could feel the grin of victory spreading over his face. He knew it wasn't Clayton's fault that, although he had finished divinity school at William and Mary, he would have to go to England to be ordained—and that was out of the question, what with the smallpox there. But it felt good to see Clayton squirm for once.

Sam clapped Thomas lightly on the shoulder. "Perhaps we should back away from the good reverend for the moment, Thomas. His blood is beginning to boil, eh?"

Suddenly, the door burst open, and Patrick's freckled face appeared. "'Tis Master Hutchinson, sir! He's comin' up the road!" he cried.

"Then we'd best get downstairs, eh?" Sam said. He cuffed Patrick playfully on the cheek and followed Clayton, who had already limped from the room, smoothing back his tawny hair with his hand. Patrick cast one careful glance at Thomas and darted after them.

But Thomas crept slowly to the window at the top of the stairs. Squinting into the pale March sun, he could see a black dot bouncing toward the house along the road. That would be Papa.

He was still so far away that Thomas had to imagine him sitting tall in the saddle, holding his head with its tri-cornered hat up high and proud. In his mind, Thomas could see the wide, square Hutchinson shoulders, the ones Sam had inherited and Clay hadn't . . . and Thomas hoped he would. And he could also picture his father's deep-set blue eyes, piercing into him, questioning why he was doing so poorly at his studies, why he was making trouble with Patrick and the other children of the servants his father had paid good money to bring from England and Scotland. He could clearly see his mouth, straightened into a disappointed line when he heard that Thomas hadn't enough energy to work at mathematics and grammar but had plenty for punching Patrick and showing disrespect for Clayton.

Thomas's eyes blurred as he watched the flapping tails of Papa's coat come into view. He knew he wouldn't be able to tell Papa why he didn't do his lessons or why the rage bristled up out of control when the other children teased him about his "feet big as fishing boats."

Butterfingered, blundering clod, he told himself miserably. *I haven't seen Papa in four months, and before that he was only two weeks home after two months gone. Why didn't I study and stay out of fights?*

Abruptly, Thomas ground his fists into his eyes to punch away the tears. *What are you crying for, sissy?* he said to himself. *Who says you have to be smart like Clayton or strong and sure like Sam? Papa barely looks at me when he's here anyhow. He's always in his library with Clayton, talking about the running of the plantation, or hovered over his desk with Samuel arguing about the war. What difference does it make what I do? Papa won't even notice.*

But the clop of a horse's hooves drove out those thoughts.

John Hutchinson dismounted and looked straight up at the window where Thomas's face was pressed.

"Good heavens!" Papa cried. "Is that my boy? Is that Thomas Hutchinson?"

Thomas stared down, frozen against the glass.

"Come down here, son!" his father called. "Come down here now. I believe we have things to talk about!"

⁑ ⸙ ⁑

y the time Thomas brushed and retied his hair, the family had Papa out of his riding coat and into a cushioned chair in the front parlor.

As he trudged unwillingly down the wide staircase, Thomas wished he was going anywhere else but to his father's side.

It *sounded* inviting. He could hear the family's laughter as he lingered in the downstairs hall. Mama's giggle that tinkled like a bell. Clayton's titter, as tight and controlled as the rest of him. Sam's confident shout-and-tumble. And Papa's hearty roar that soared above all the rest, yet still sounded like a gentleman.

That will all stop the minute Papa starts to question me, he thought.

As Thomas slipped into the parlor, Mattie, the kitchen maid, was moving a tray from the tea cart to the table in the center, and all eyes were locked on to the array of cakes and tarts whose sugared tops sparkled in the light from the fireplace.

Perhaps I can slide into a seat without anyone noticing, Thomas thought. Keeping his gaze glued on Papa, he silently sidestepped toward a chair at the edge of the room. On the third step, his thigh met something hard, and before he could catch himself, he toppled over onto the floor. With a crash, a flood of cups and saucers and silver spoons showered down on him. When he put up his arm to shield his face, something warm and wet splashed onto his clean white shirt and soaked it through to his skin.

"Thomas!" he heard his mother cry. "John, he'll be scalded! That's hot cocoa!"

Thomas tried to scramble up, but two hands brought him to his feet. Thomas looked up into the piercing blue eyes of his father.

There was a long and terrible moment while Papa studied his face. No one spoke—they seldom did when Papa had The Look. It was the one with the heavy, dust-colored eyebrows knitted in thought, the mouth pressed grimly into a stern line, and the eyes drilling into the poor soul he was looking at. Most often, he lowered it on his sons.

Has Clayton already told him all the trouble I've been in these last four months? Thomas thought wildly. *What is to be done with me?*

Tears were threatening at the back of Thomas's throat, when suddenly the grim line across Papa's face softened and absently he patted Thomas's shoulder. His eyes were already drifting away as he said, "See that you help pick up the mess you've made now."

"And afterward, go change your shirt, Thomas," Mama added softly. Then her eyes riveted back to Papa, too.

Hello! Thomas wanted to say. *I'm still here. I'm part of the family, too!*

But when no one gave him a second glance, Thomas crawled under the table for a cup that had rolled there and chewed at the inside of his mouth. At least Papa hadn't begun to interrogate him about his behavior. Wasn't this what he'd hoped for anyway, to remain unnoticed?

Thomas wasn't sure. He only knew he could feel the anger bristling up on the back of his neck again. Where was Patrick? He needed someone to punch.

Above him, the conversation went on as if everyone had been interrupted by an annoying fly for a moment and then forgotten it at once.

"I think it was a mistake to move the capitol to Richmond," Papa was saying. "Before he was governor, Thomas Jefferson used to say that Williamsburg was the finest place of manners and morals in America."

Sam grunted. "You wouldn't think so today. Since the government left, it's nothing but a dumpy, boring town with ruts for roads—and a bunch of Loyalists still living there."

Papa went on as if Sam hadn't spoken. "Now Jefferson thinks he and the Virginia government will be safer in Richmond, but I disagree. Clinton has his eye on Richmond, that's for certain. He thinks the South is full of Tories who will help him."

"What are Tories, John?" Mama cut in quickly.

"Tories and Loyalists are almost the same thing, my dear," Papa said. "They both support the British in this madness. So far, we've been fortunate that the fighting has stayed up north for the most part. But they're in a stalemate there. The war will be moving south, you mark my words."

"And who is Clinton?" Mama said. Thomas could imagine her big gray eyes shimmering as she watched her husband out of the ring of dark curls that circled her face.

"Clinton is in command of the King's army," Papa said. "He sits cozy in New York, keeping himself and his soldiers warm and well fed. Ours have just spent a horrible winter at Valley Forge. They had tents pitched on frozen ground and slept under straw. We barely have enough men to carry on, and very little ammunition and guns—"

"But Father!" Sam cried.

As Thomas stood up to put his stack of cups back on the tea cart, he stole a glance at Sam. His brother was leaning forward on his chair.

"The British may have more men and guns and experience, but we Americans *believe* in our cause and that can make all the difference! They have to *beat* us in order to win, because we aren't going to surrender!"

"Poppycock, Samuel!" Papa said brusquely. "There has to be a peaceful way to settle this thing—to rule ourselves and still remain British subjects."

"It's too late for that!" Sam said, his handsome face going red. "We've had the Articles of Confederation since 1778. That's a permanent agreement among the colonies that we are our own nation."

Papa stood up and marched to the window. "The war for independence is a miserable affair," he said. "And we would all have been better off if it had never been started."

Clayton sniffed in agreement. "When it all began in Lexington and Concord, everyone said we would be independent from England within the year." He gave a short laugh. "That was five years ago next month."

"General Washington will come south," Sam said, as if he had talked to George Washington only that afternoon. Thomas looked at him with admiration. Sam always seemed to just *know* things.

"I don't know what good that will do," Papa said.

"Savannah and Augusta have already fallen to the British in Georgia."

"But I've heard that there are ruthless Patriots down there," Sam pressed on excitedly. "Not men who stand shoulder to shoulder with rifles and go into battle, but guerrillas who come out of the swamps and fight like Americans." His blue eyes sparked. "That's what I want to do."

"You'll do nothing of the kind!" Papa said. "You'll finish your schooling—"

Sam came up out of his chair, setting several teacups tottering. "Why am I not allowed to fight for what I believe in?"

"You don't know what you believe yet," his father said. "You're flaming up like a firebrand!"

"Father, I want to be part of this. It's going to be my country!"

"There won't be a country left to have if we all kill each other! Look what has happened already. We are now constantly fighting our own battles with our Loyalist neighbors!"

"Are you talking about Carter Ludwell, John?" Mama asked.

"I am! I never cared much for him personally, but at least I could pass him in Yorktown or Williamsburg without him needling me with his petty complaints."

"I have yet to tell you about his latest one," Clayton said.

"We should run Loyalists like Ludwell out of Virginia!" Sam said. "If they're not for us, then they're against us."

"Samuel!"

The room went dead and all eyes went to their laps. The only thing worse than Papa's Look was his Tone, Thomas knew. And he was using it now. It was quiet . . . and heavy as a stone.

"There will be no more talk of running the Loyalists out. I have already proposed a policy in Williamsburg that Loyalists be treated the same as everyone else until such time as we are legally independent. I expect you all to support me on this."

Sam grunted and moved to the outskirts of the room.

"More tarts anyone?" Mama said.

Papa waved the tray away and sat back sullenly in his seat.

Now would be a good time for me to escape, Thomas thought.

He began to edge toward the door. Mama asked Papa what the ladies were wearing in Richmond. Mattie refilled a few teacups. No one glanced his way. Thomas stopped.

I could probably leave the plantation altogether and no one would notice, he thought, his neck bristling again. *No one really cares what I do.*

Again, Thomas wanted to punch someone . . . or throw something . . . or shout at somebody. Mattie chose that moment to pass him with the cluttered cart and whisper, "Run along and change your shirt like your Mama said."

"No!" Thomas said through his teeth.

"Now Master Thomas—"

"Leave me alone! I'll go when I please, you wretched witch!"

Mattie gaped at him, her mouth open. Around her, silence roared in the parlor.

It was broken by a shout that made Thomas tremble from top to toe.

"*What* is the meaning of this?" Papa cried out. "What do you mean by behaving in such a fashion?"

John Hutchinson's fiery eyes were demanding a reply, but

Thomas couldn't say a word. He couldn't even shake his head.

Papa stood and towered over him in fury, but Thomas still couldn't move.

Papa gave a snort of disgust and turned on Clayton.

"What is this?" he said to Clayton. "Has he been behaving like this since I put him in your charge?"

"Yes, sir, he has," Clayton said.

"Tell me straight, and tell me everything. I demand to know."

Thomas felt as if the shiny parlor floor was slowly sinking into the ground and taking him with it. There was nothing he could do now except wait for it to swallow him completely.

"He treats the servants' children like that all the time," Clayton said. "They have only to look at him cross-eyed and he's on them like a crazed bear."

"And his studies?" Papa said sharply.

"He's made very little progress, sir," Clayton said. "He refuses to set his mind to learning anything except how to throw a punch. I have tried everything, sir. He's stubborn as a bull."

The whole parlor seemed to be holding its breath as Papa looked deep into Thomas's face.

Thomas's eyes went to the floor. *Not only do I have Papa looking at me as if I were the biggest disappointment of his life*, he thought, *but I have everyone else here watching him do it*. The hair stood up on the back of his neck, and he clenched his fists hard at his sides. Before he could stop it, his mouth flew open.

"Clayton is a liar!" Thomas cried out. "And he's a rotten teacher as well! But you'll never believe me, Father, so do what you want with me!"

Thomas's eyes flashed across the parlor. The faces that met his were all stiff with disbelief. Before they could recover, he shoved past Mattie and tore toward the stairs.

Facedown on his bed, Thomas cried until his throat ached and no more tears would come. Then he lay there, biting his feather pillow.

Don't cry anymore, sissy, he told himself harshly. *They are none of them worth it anyway. Let them send me away. I hope they send me away.*

But that thought hurt more than anything that had happened today.

The Hutchinson Homestead was all he'd ever known. Except for the occasional trip into Williamsburg, a dozen miles away, his whole life had centered around this plantation and the docks at Yorktown, where his father's company built ships.

Until this year, it had been a peaceful life. Esther, his plump gray-haired nanny, had taught him the basic things he'd needed to know, and his mother had bought him toys and let him have treats and told him what a fine boy he was. Not much had been expected of him, and he'd lived a life of doing almost exactly as he pleased.

He hadn't seen much of Papa since the war had started five years ago, but Mama always assured him that his father was thinking about him. He just had important business to do to keep the colony of Virginia running.

And then Clayton had come home from college in Williamsburg last year. He was finished with divinity school and there was nothing for him to do while he waited for a chance to be ordained—while he prayed for a bishop to be sent to the Virginia colony from England to do it. Nothing, that is, except run the plantation for Papa while he went off to Richmond. And that included gathering Thomas and the children of Papa's indentured servants together and teaching them reading, writing, mathematics, and religion. That was when everything had changed—all at once.

Clayton acted as if he thought he were supposed to take Papa's place in Thomas's life. Thomas hated being told what to do by his older brother, and yet Clayton seemed to be everywhere, even in church.

Thomas had always gone to Grace Church in Yorktown with the family, even when Papa was gone, and Mama had allowed him to bring a small toy to amuse himself while the service dragged on. But when Clayton appeared, he had to sit as if he had a pole up his back and listen to every word so Clayton could quiz him over Sunday dinner. Week after week, roast duck or baked ham had gone dry in his mouth as Clayton had fired questions at him that he refused to answer.

And as if that weren't enough, suddenly it seemed like he was tripping over everything, as if pieces of furniture were jumping out in front of him and sprawling him to the ground at every turn. That's when the teasing and taunting started from the other children. He couldn't hold back anymore. When the anger prickled the back of his neck, there was nothing to do but punch.

It was easy to do. He was bigger than Patrick and the other boys, even though some were older. He'd watched the blood trickle out of their noses more than once.

And I don't care, he told himself fiercely. *I don't care how much they hurt. I hurt, too!*

He flopped himself over on his feather bed and faced the

door with his jaw set. It creaked open and Sam's face appeared in the dim light.

"Thomas, are you awake?" he whispered.

"Yes." Thomas sat up eagerly and wiped quickly at his eyes. "Come in!"

But Sam stayed in the doorway and shook his head. "No such luck, little brother," he said. "Your appointment is with your father—in his library—in five minutes."

Thomas heard himself gasp, and Sam nodded slowly.

"I would be quivering in my boots, too, if I were you. I'm afraid I haven't gotten him in a very good mood for you."

"What do you mean?"

"In the library just now we continued this afternoon's session."

"Oh," Thomas said. "More of The Look?"

"Yes, and more of The Tone. The man grows more stubborn as he gets older." Sam gave a hard laugh. "And so do I. I will win, just you wait and see."

Thomas gazed in awe at his brother. *I wonder if I'll ever be as sure and strong and smart as Sam*, he thought wistfully.

"You'd better pull yourself together," Sam said. "Just take what he gives you and don't argue."

"Is that what you would do?" Thomas said.

Sam shrugged. "No," he said. "But you're not me."

-✝- -✚- -✝-

Chapter Three

Papa's library had always been one of Thomas's favorite rooms in the plantation mansion, perhaps because it smelled so much like his father. The leather-bound books. The pot of ink on the desk. The steam of hot apple cider. The scent of Papa himself—a little bit of sweat, a little bit of horse soap, a little bit of lilac water.

But all Thomas could smell that night as he approached the library door to face his father was dread—a little bit of his own sweat, a little bit of the tears he'd just wiped from his cheeks, a little bit of the blood he'd drawn from biting hard on the inside of his mouth.

Just as he was about to knock on the big mahogany door, he heard voices from inside. Thomas stepped back from the door and listened.

"We have been neighbors all our lives, Carter," Papa was saying. "Why suddenly do you think I am out to rob you blind?"

"Because you're a Patriot and I'm a Loyalist, that's why!" the other voice cried.

Thomas recognized it as Carter Ludwell's voice. He owned the plantation nearest to theirs.

"My political beliefs have nothing to do with this!" said John Hutchinson. "I believe in freedom, not thievery!"

"You're out to get me, Hutchinson, and you can't deny it."

"I can and I do. I insist that you leave."

Papa's voice had grown so low that Thomas could barely hear him, and he moved forward to get his ear closer to the door. When it suddenly flew open, it caught him squarely in the chest and knocked him across the hall.

He looked up to see Carter Ludwell stomping off, his wiry little arms pumping at his sides.

"Thomas?"

Thomas scrambled up. His father was standing in the doorway. "Come in, please."

In the library, he nodded toward a blue wing-back chair that faced his desk, and Thomas slipped into it obediently. If it had been any other occasion, he would have proudly noticed that his feet touched the floor when he sat in it.

John Hutchinson perched on the front edge of his desk and picked up a stone that had rested on the desktop ever since Thomas could remember. While Thomas's heart thundered in his ears, his father examined the stone as if he'd never seen it before. He looked at it for so long that Thomas had to bite his mouth again to keep from crying out, "Please, sir, let's get on with it!"

"Have I ever told you about this stone?" Papa said finally.

The stone? Thomas thought. *What about* me?

"My great-grandfather—your great-great-grandfather—Joseph Hutchinson brought this with him in 1692 from Massachusetts. That's where he was born and where the Hutchinson family first landed in America."

He passed the stone to Thomas. It was a small, smooth stone that lay comfortably in his palm. When he turned it over, he saw the drawing of a wolf on it, faint now after years of being held in Hutchinson hands. Thomas looked at his father blankly.

"What do you make of it?" Papa asked.

Thomas shrugged. "I suppose it's important."

"You suppose correctly," said Papa. "It's important because it represents the Hutchinson tradition. My grandfather told me that when Josiah, your great-grandfather, was just a boy, he was given this stone by an Indian woman. He later learned that to the Indians, the wolf is a reminder that it is our job to be leaders. Josiah gave the stone to his father, Joseph. And when Joseph Hutchinson saw fit to leave Massachusetts and come to Virginia, he was a leader of men. First he established this plantation—300 acres of some of the best land in the entire area."

Thomas nodded vaguely and fidgeted in the chair. What did all of this have to do with the trouble he was in?

"And then Josiah Hutchinson took it one step further. He started his own shipping line so that not only could he sell the goods he grew here, but he could trade with ports other than England. Are you listening to me?"

"Yes, sir!" Thomas said quickly.

"*His* son, my father—Daniel Hutchinson—built up the docks in Yorktown. And he purchased 300 more acres so he could rotate his crops and not wear out the land. I have tried to follow in his footsteps. When others insisted that tobacco was the only crop Virginia could produce, I continued to grow wheat. I have kept our fortune alive while others flounder because their tobacco ruins the land for years and because they can trade only with England, which refuses to trade with us now."

He stared at Thomas and continued. "When others began to buy slaves, I continued on with indentured servants. I paid

for their way to the Virginia colony, where they've worked for
me until I've been repaid by their services—and then I let
them go to make their own fortunes. I have sacrificed being
elected to the House of Burgesses—the governing body of the
very colony my family has helped to build—and have served
only as an aide to those who were elected, because I have
differed in these philosophies with my fellow planters. But I
am fiercely proud of what Joseph, Josiah, Daniel, and I have
done. We represent a great tradition here in Virginia."

Papa leaned toward Thomas and put his hand out for the
stone. As Thomas dropped it into his palm, he saw The Look
appear on his father's face. "I thought I had raised my sons to
carry on that tradition," Papa said. "In your case, it seems I
was wrong."

Thomas stared down into his lap at the smudged, nail-
bitten hands that were clasped there. Anger was creeping up
the back of his neck, but tears were gathering behind his eye-
lids, too. He didn't know whether to lash out like a whip or
cry like a baby. And he was too afraid to do either.

He watched as Papa's silver-buckled shoes paced up and
down in front of him. It seemed his father would wear a path
in the rug before he stopped and reached down to tilt
Thomas's chin toward him.

"It isn't too late, Thomas," Papa said. "But in order for
you to carry on the Hutchinson name, you're going to need
more careful looking after than you've had. Your mother and
Esther have spoiled you, and Clayton doesn't have a strong
enough will to deal with you." He stopped and leaned back on
the desk again. "If we win this war against England, you can
be sure many things will change. Every man in America will
have to work even harder to keep the fine life we have made

for ourselves here. And that includes you." John Hutchinson stabbed a finger toward Thomas. "And you are no more ready for it than one of our newborn calves."

Thomas let out a long sigh of relief. This lecture wasn't any worse than anything Clayton had held over his head up in the schoolroom.

Papa stood up suddenly and went behind his desk to pick up a sheaf of papers. "So," he said briskly, "since no one else in this house is able to prepare you for what lies ahead, I am taking matters into my own hands. This," he said, as he waved the papers, "is the deed to the house I have purchased in Williamsburg. The government of Virginia must rely on the support of the rest of the colony, and I have been asked to act as a link with Williamsburg. It will be necessary for me to spend most of my time there, so I am leaving Clayton in full charge of the plantation, and I am taking you and your mother to live with me."

Thomas's heart lurched. "I'm to be moved to Williamsburg?"

"Indeed you are. I want you where I can keep a closer eye on your progress. I have not yet worked out the details, but I plan to obtain a private tutor for you to get you to the place where you ought to be with your studies. You stand no chance of entering the grammar school at William and Mary at the rate you're going."

"But—"

"And you can count on taking a large share of the responsibility for the work that must be done to keep the household running. I cannot afford to take too many servants away from their work here. Only Esther and Otis will go with us."

Esther and Otis? Thomas wailed to himself as his father droned on. *They can barely make it up the stairs anymore! I'll be worked to death!*

His father shot him a warning glance. "Have you some problem with that?"

"No," Thomas lied.

"Good. You are so far behind where you should be as a young man that it will only be by the grace of God that I get you there. I thank Him that I have caught you in time."

Then John Hutchinson looked down at the papers on his desk, and Thomas knew the conversation was over. At least for his father. But the back of Thomas's neck was stiff with anger. There was certainly more *he* wanted to say. . . .

"If you're thinking you would like to argue any of this with me, Thomas, you'd best think again." His father was leaning with both hands on the desk. "My mind is made up. You will not mar the Hutchinson name, nor will you waste the life the Lord has given you being stubborn and selfish. Not if I have anything to do with it—and I promise you, son, I do."

And with that, the conversation was over.

When Thomas awoke the next morning, he knew he had never spent a more miserable night in his 10 and a half years.

He'd lain in the middle of the four poster bed for hours with only a pale sliver of a moon to listen to him as he muttered all the things he'd wanted to say to his father.

You can't take me away from Hutchinson Homestead. This is my home. This is where I belong.

I don't know anyone in Williamsburg. They'll all think I'm a bumbling fool. They'll make fun of me, and I'll have to fight them.

And work in the house? I don't know how to do anything! How can I chop firewood and scrub floors?

Study with a real teacher?

At that point, Thomas had sat up in bed with his arms crossed and his square jaw set.

Well, his thoughts had sputtered, *you can hire a tutor, but you can't make me learn. I won't have anyone proving that I am not as smart as Clayton and Sam.*

He'd punched and bitten his pillow until feathers escaped in clumps. The moon was long gone by the time he fell into a troubled sleep.

When he woke up, everything was just the same—the sun trying to make its way past his heavy, blue drapes, the smells of johnny cakes and mush and pumpkin bread wafting up from the dining room, and Esther bustling around his room, picking up his shirts and stockings and grumbling to herself. It was as if the day before had been nothing but a dream.

But with a jerk, the blue drapes came open, and thin March sunlight glared into the room. That's when Thomas knew it hadn't been a nightmare at all. There was already a trunk open beside his clothes press, and Esther was tottering toward it with an armful of his breeches.

Thomas sat upright in the bed and tore off the covers. He was headed for Esther before his bare feet even touched the floor.

"What are you doing with my clothes?"

He reached out to grab the pile, but old Esther deftly pulled it out of his reach and dropped the pants into the open trunk.

"I'm a-goin' to Williamsburg with them, that's what I'm doin'," she said. She gave the quick little nod of her gray head she used to punctuate the end of every sentence. "And so are you."

Thomas stamped his foot and yanked a pair of breeches

out of the trunk, tossing them over his shoulder. "I'm not!"

Esther clicked her tongue as she picked them up, but Thomas didn't miss the mist in her eyes. "Don't you think I hate to leave this place as much as you do? Worked here all my life, I have. Nursed your father here, I did, and grew up with your grandfather. We sat in a schoolroom together."

"Then you should stay here . . . and so should I!"

Esther bobbed her head harder than ever. "I don't think your tantrums and your fits are a-goin' to get you anywhere this time. I think you've finally run into someone who's twice as stubborn as you are."

It turned out that Esther was right. Two days later, the trunk, his mother, Esther, Otis—and Thomas—all piled into the Hutchinson carriage with Papa and trotted off to Williamsburg.

Thomas squeezed miserably inside the carriage beside Esther, across from his parents, and gazed back at Hutchinson Homestead with a strange ache in his chest.

Clayton stood on the front porch with Mattie and their cook, while Patrick and some of the other children chased the carriage down the road lined with tulip poplars. As many times as he had pouted at Clayton, or snapped at Mattie, or socked Patrick's jaw, watching them shrink into tiny dots was like having a stick poked into his heart.

I hate them for staying there when I have to go to boring Williamsburg, Thomas grumbled to himself.

The anger sneaked up the back of his neck, and he sighed. There. That felt better than the pain in his chest.

The road to Williamsburg was muddy from the spring thaw, and they bounced and jounced over the ruts so hard that Thomas's bottom came right up off the seat. The only sounds were the creaking of the carriage and Otis crooning to the four horses. That was the only time Otis ever made a sound. Esther did all the talking for him.

"Now, Master Hutchinson," she said as they left the Homestead far behind. "Tell me again why you're working in Williamsburg now."

Papa smiled. "You're a nosy one, aren't you, Esther? I'm to help the town uphold the laws of our new state so that the colony can remain united until this war is over and our nation is independent. My biggest job will be to make sure that there is no trouble between the Loyalists and the Patriots as there has been in New England."

Esther bobbed her head. "Now mind you, I know nothin' about it. But I don't trust those Loyalists, not for a minute."

"Nor do I, Esther," Papa said soothingly. "Some of them can be downright evil. But they have their rights, just like the rest of us."

Mama nervously smoothed her skirts. "I certainly hope that Carter Ludwell isn't going to make trouble for Clayton while you're gone."

"The Hutchinsons have nothing to fear from Carter Ludwell or anyone else, my dear," Papa said. "We are decent, godly people."

Except for me, Thomas thought glumly. *I've already been told I'm about as decent as one of our calves.*

He bit the inside of his mouth and glared out the window.

Before long, the damp, naked trees and thawing marshes were joined by houses and stables and woodsheds. Papa took Mama's hand.

"We're nearly there," he said. "If you'll all keep watch, you'll see Williamsburg appear."

Am I supposed to give a cheer? Thomas thought. *Sam says it's muddy and empty and boring here—and I believe him.*

But Papa found it all delightful, and he pointed out every landmark as they turned with a lurch onto the Duke of Gloucester Street, which ran right through the center of town.

"The street is over a mile long and a hundred feet wide," Papa said proudly. "On this end is the Capitol Building, you see—deserted now—and behind it the jail."

"Oh," Mama said with a shudder.

"There's the millinery. You'll find fine hats in there, my dear. And there's the silversmith and the apothecary—"

"Good," said Esther. "I'll need to know where to get medicine."

"That's the Raleigh Tavern where I often take my meals for business purposes," Papa went on. "Now, we're coming upon the County Courthouse, and you'll see the Market Square across the street. Market Day is every Wednesday, Esther. Ah, now next, just where we're going to turn to go up the Palace Green, you see Bruton Parish Church. That's where we'll be attending services."

Thomas tried not to groan as he looked at the brick church with its round window on the end and its steeple that poked up through the bare trees. Going to church had been bad enough when he had to sit next to Clayton. What was his father going to require of him?

"Now," Papa was saying, "up on the rise there you see the mill, which is where we have always taken our grain, and straight ahead at the end of this lovely green—"

Lovely? Thomas thought. *It's muddy, and there are sheep grazing on it!*

"—is the Governor's Palace. Since Thomas Jefferson left, it has stood empty."

"What a shame," Mama said. "It was always grand inside."

Thomas stared at it. It was just a naked brick mansion with an empty white tower on top.

"You always did love elegance, my dear," Papa said to his wife. "Unfortunately, I don't think you'll find our little Williamsburg house will quite measure up to that."

Otis stopped the carriage in front of a square, brick house with two chimneys sticking up out of its roof like goat's horns. To Thomas, it looked stiff and plain, like a larger version of their servants' quarters on the plantation.

"This is our new home," Papa said.

"I think it will do just fine," Esther said.

"John, it's charming!" Mama said.

"I hate it," Thomas said.

Papa turned and pierced his blue eyes straight through him. Thomas bit his lip and followed everyone inside.

While Mama let out ooh's and ahh's and Esther bustled Otis off to find the kitchen building, Thomas took his own survey.

No grand curved staircase or main hallway paneled in pine. Just a narrow set of stairs that led up into darkness.

No terraced lawns and brick stables. Just neglected gardens and clapboard outbuildings—a stable, chicken house, lumber house, smokehouse, laundry, and kitchen.

No marble mantle or carved mahogany paneling or silver and crystal on the dining room sideboard. No fine carpets or ornaments imported from Europe. No Chippendale furniture.

Just plain and dismal, just as Sam had said it would be.

"I'll begin at once to make this a home," Mama said.

"No," said Papa. "First we must gather in the parlor and have a service of Evening Prayer. We must thank God for our safe journey and our new home."

Everyone's face, even Otis's, seemed to light up at the thought of doing church right there in the house. At dusk, when the Bruton Parish Church bells rang, the five of them met, and Papa opened his worn copy of the *Book of Common Prayer*.

"'O, worship the Lord in the beauty of holiness,'" Papa read. "'Let the whole earth stand in awe of Him.'"

Thomas stood, but it wasn't in awe. He fidgeted in his sleeves and poked his toes at the planks of the hardwood floor until Papa read "'The grace of our Lord Jesus Christ, and the love of God, and the fellowship of the Holy Ghost be with us all evermore. Amen,'" and closed the book.

Esther's eyes were practically overflowing as she ushered Thomas upstairs to get ready for bed.

"I don't see what all the fuss is about," Thomas said.

"Your father used to pray Evening Prayer with the family every evening before the war started," she told him. "You just don't remember." She bobbed her head several times. "It touched my heart to be a-prayin' it again."

It didn't touch my heart, Thomas thought.

He climbed into his new bed and felt its lumps under his back.

"I just want to go home," he whispered out loud. "Please let me go home."

✛ ✛ ✛

Chapter Four

"**T**homas!" Mama's voice rang up the stairs like a chain of silver bells. "Get your school things and come downstairs now," she called out. "Master Alexander will be here any minute!"

Thomas shrugged and slunk to the window of his room that overlooked the deserted Palace Green. It was bad enough that Williamsburg was downright boring. But now his life here was about to get even worse. "Master Alexander" was on his way to start tutoring Thomas.

Some old geezer with whiskers poking out of his chin, no doubt, Thomas thought.

He kicked at the post on his bed—a bed that was as lumpy as Esther's mush.

And that was another thing. Esther couldn't cook like Mattie and Cookie. There was no stockpile of good food here as there was on the plantation, and Papa had explained that most of the things they enjoyed—such as sugar, molasses, and raisins—were impossible to get now that England had cut off the colonies from receiving goods.

Thomas needed good food, he'd whined to Esther, what with the appetite he was working up before every meal. In the week they'd been in Williamsburg, he had stoked fires, made beds, cleaned rooms, and swept the sidewalk. He'd even emptied chamber pots.

Those were things he had watched the servant children do since he himself was old enough to walk—only they did them so easily. Thomas didn't even want to think about the number of times he'd stumbled and fallen with water buckets or loads of wood in his hands this past week.

Only two good things had happened to him since he'd been there, he decided now.

The first was that Sam had come for supper one night. He seemed to understand Thomas's misery, and he sympathized.

"I know how you feel. I can't wait to leave this town myself and go off to fight in the war," he'd whispered to Thomas.

But even that visit had grown dreary when Papa and Sam argued again about Sam's leaving school to become a soldier.

The second good thing was that Papa had been so busy setting up his office in the back of the house that he hadn't had time to lecture Thomas.

"I'd give anything to be back at the Homestead, even if it meant never seeing Papa again," Thomas said out loud to no one.

But suddenly there *was* someone, hurrying up the avenue with a large satchel.

He was a young man—maybe as old as Clayton—with honey-colored hair brushed back from his face and curled around his ears. He was obviously in a hurry, what with his celery-colored coat flying out behind him as he opened the gate in front of the Hutchinson house and hastened up the steps.

Someone for Papa, Thomas thought.

There was a tap at his bedroom door, followed by Esther's mob-capped head poking in.

"Your mama sent me to tell you that Master Alexander is

arrived," she said, bobbing her head for emphasis.

"How could he be?" Thomas asked. "I didn't see him come to the door."

Esther put her hands on her rather wide hips. "Just because you didn't see him doesn't mean he isn't right downstairs in the dinin' room a-spreadin' out his teachin' things this very minute." She gave two head bobs this time and walked stiffly out of the room, muttering, "Stubbornest boy I ever saw. The Lord bless this schoolmaster, or the boy'll run him right back where he came from."

Thomas stared after her.

Run him back where he came from, she'd said.

That's a good idea, Thomas thought. He could almost feel a gleam coming into his eyes.

Thomas's head was already full of plans for a worm in Master Alexander's inkwell when he jolted to a halt at the dining room door. There, spreading out books and quill pens, was the young man with the honey-colored hair and the celery-colored coat. Thomas squared his jaw.

"This is not my father's office," he said importantly.

The young man looked up at him blankly. "It isn't?"

Thomas shook his head. "Back of the house. He'll be wondering where you are."

"Will he now?"

"That's right. He doesn't like for people to be late."

The young man laced his fingers together under his chin. "Should I be worried then?"

Thomas felt himself smile slyly. "I would be, were I you," he said.

"And who *are* you, since you aren't me?"

It was only then that Thomas realized he was being made fun of. His hackles stood up, and he straightened his shoulders to his full height. "I'm Thomas Hutchinson—his *son*," he said.

The young man stuck out his hand and smiled until a deep dimple appeared in each cheek. "Just the man I wanted to see! I'm Alexander, your tutor!"

Thomas almost let his jaw drop before he caught himself. "*You?*" he said. "Why didn't you say so?"

"Just did," Alexander said.

Thomas thought hard. He'd better take control right from the beginning if he were going to—what was it Esther had said?—run this poor man back where he came from.

He pulled out one of the mahogany side chairs he had just polished the day before and slouched in it, arms folded across his chest. He studied the teacher carefully, but except for one dimple indenting his left cheek, Alexander just looked back.

"How can you be a real teacher?" Thomas said finally. "You're too young."

"Am I?" Alexander said. "How old am I?"

Thomas rolled his eyes. "How am I to know?"

"Well, if you don't know, how can you say I'm too young?"

Thomas's neck stiffened, and he sat up a little. "You don't look much older than my brother Sam."

"How old is he?"

"Sixteen."

"You're right. I'm not much older. Eighteen years, two months, to be exact. Looks *can* be deceiving."

Thomas frowned. "What do you mean?"

"Your father tells me you're only 10. By the size of you, I'd have guessed you to be at least 12."

Thomas puffed out his chest for a minute, but then he caught himself again.

"If you're 18 and healthy," he said. "Why aren't you in the Continental Army with George Washington, fighting for the colonies?"

"How do you know I'm healthy?"

"You look—"

"Ah! Caught you again! I told you, looks can be deceiving. But don't feel too badly. I only told you once. To really learn something, the average boy has to hear it at least 20 times."

Alexander wasn't folding his arms or planting his hands on his hips or any of the other I'm-the-mighty-teacher-you're-the-lowly-student things Clayton always did. But still Thomas bristled.

"How do you know I'm the average boy?" he asked.

Alexander scrunched up his eyes and sprayed laughter all over the table.

"What's so funny?" Thomas said, scowling.

"Me!" Alexander said. "I thought you were an 'average boy,' but I stand corrected. I wouldn't be surprised if you could beat me at my own game."

You bet I will, Thomas thought.

But his thoughts trailed off as Alexander reached into his book satchel and pulled out three balls—one red, one yellow, and one blue. He tossed the red to Thomas, but by the time he got his arms untangled, it had flown toward the fireplace, and Thomas was grasping for empty air.

"Good try!" Alexander said. "Perhaps you can fetch it from the hearth there, eh?"

"I'm not a dog," Thomas muttered to himself, but he stumbled over and retrieved the ball. As soon as he turned around with it, Alexander pitched him the blue one. Thomas grabbed at it with his other hand, dropping the red ball, missing the blue, and tripping over one of the mahogany chairs as he lunged for both of them.

"Why are we playing ball?" Thomas grumbled as he crawled under the table. "We're supposed to be studying."

As Thomas emerged from under the table, Alexander leaned over to look at him eye to eye. "But we *are* studying, Thomas Hutchinson. Now stand up." He helped Thomas to his feet. "Perhaps we should start with one. Put the blue one on the table, and toss the red one in the air and catch—"

The ball skittered across the rug, and Thomas could feel his face burning.

"Not such a high altitude this time, eh?" Alexander said. "Just toss it lightly." Thomas followed the instructions. "There you have it. Now again. Good. You've got the hang of it. Now, pick up the blue, and holding the red one in your hand, toss the blue up and catch it."

Thomas held his breath. *Please*, he thought. *Let me catch this so I don't look the fool in front of this tyrant.*

Thomas was never sure when he had thoughts like that exactly who he was talking to, but whoever it was listened this time because he watched the blue ball carefully and it landed in his palm.

"Ah! Splendid!" Alexander said.

He looked so genuinely pleased that Thomas had to furrow his brows furiously to keep from feeling pleased himself. After all, most babies could toss a ball up and catch it. What was all the fuss about? This Alexander person was surely mocking him.

"Now what?" Thomas said, voice prickling.

"Ah, now it becomes more difficult, but I am convinced you can master this, young Hutchinson. Listen carefully. Toss the red ball up and while it's in the air, toss the blue one up, and catch the red one and toss it before the blue one comes back down."

Thomas sniffed. "Oh. That looks easy."

"Good, then. Try it."

Thomas sent the red ball into the air and then the blue one. The red immediately popped him on the head, and as he groped for it, the blue fell lamely to the floor and rolled toward the sideboard.

"Ah, those looks continue to be deceiving, don't they? But not to worry. Pick them up and try it once more. Slowly this time, and keep your eye on the ball that's in the air."

Thomas chomped at his mouth, but he riveted his eyes to the red ball as it sailed crazily over his head. Once more turned into six more times. On the seventh, both balls returned safely to his hands, and beads of sweat dotted Thomas's upper lip.

"Are you ready to add a third—the dreaded yellow?" Alexander asked.

Thomas shrugged. "If it pleases you."

"Ah, it does. It does indeed. Nothing pleases a teacher more than to see a student learning."

Suddenly, another voice filled the room. "And what is it he is supposed to be learning?"

Thomas's eyes whipped to the doorway, and at once he felt that thrill of victory.

There stood his father—with The Look on his face . . . aimed at Alexander.

⚜ ⚜ ⚜

Chapter Five

"**M**r. Hutchinson!" Alexander said.

Thomas sat back down in the chair and fixed his attention on Papa. He didn't want to miss watching John Hutchinson send the teacher "back where he came from."

"I had thought to come and report to you when I arrived," Alexander was saying, "but your wife said you were busy, so I came in here straightaway and got to work with young Thomas."

Papa's heavy eyebrows drew closer together. "It looked more like play to me."

Thomas had to lock his hands behind his back to keep from rubbing them together in glee. *Talk yourself out of this one, Teacher*, he thought happily.

"Do you take pleasure in reading a fine book, Mr. Hutchinson?" Alexander said.

"Why, yes, but—"

"Then learning has become like play to you. I see no reason why learning has to be drudgery for Thomas."

Thomas waited in delicious anticipation. Here it came. No one said such ridiculous things to John Hutchinson and stayed around long.

"Of course," Alexander said, "if you would rather, I will

37

stay with more traditional methods, Mr. Hutchinson."

"No, no," Papa said. "I find this quite interesting. Please, carry on. I should like to observe for a while."

Alexander shined his eyes at Thomas. "Shall we demonstrate for your father?"

But Thomas was still staring at Papa, chin dropped to his chest. Had he heard right? Had Papa just failed to toss this fake teacher out into the street? How could he have missed the fact that Alexander was toying with them both?

Papa pulled a chair to the edge of the room and sat down, while Alexander picked up all three balls and began to toss them, lightly and evenly, catching each one as if it were as easy as breathing.

"This," he said as he juggled, "is what we shall work on next, Thomas. It looks simple, and it is for me now, but it won't be for you at first. You must simply concentrate and work slowly."

With each of his last words, he tossed a ball up in the air and caught it.

You had to show off for Papa, didn't you, Master Alexander? Thomas thought angrily. *You had to make sure he noticed how smart and sure you are, so it will be so much more clear how stupid and clumsy I am.*

Thomas glared at the balls waiting to be scattered all over the floor with his father watching. What was the use? He would never be like Alexander—or Clayton or Sam—so why even try? And if he did try—and failed—Papa would know for sure that his youngest son was useless after all.

"Well, Thomas," Alexander said. "Will you give it a go?"

"No," Thomas said.

Alexander blinked. "No? Why not?"

"Because it's stupid. I could do it if I wanted . . . but I don't want to."

How do you like that, Alexander? he added in his mind. *Now* you *will be the one to look the fool in front of John Hutchinson.*

"Catch!" Alexander cried. The red ball came toward Thomas, and in spite of himself he grabbed it from the air, just as the blue one joined it and landed in his palm. When the yellow ball sailed his way, it bounced off his chest and tumbled to the floor. Thomas watched it roll and then looked in surprise at the two balls in his hands. Alexander had tricked him. He'd been about to try this silly juggling thing after all.

With a heave, Thomas thrust both balls onto the floor and snarled up at his tutor.

"I said I won't play your wretched game!"

"And I tell you you will," his father said quietly. His voice sent a chill up the back of Thomas's neck. "But not today. Go back up to your room now. I shall send for you later."

Thomas didn't have to be told twice. He plunged toward the door, only to feel a large hand on his shoulder.

"But first," his father said, "pick up those balls and return them to Master Alexander."

Thomas whirled around, his mouth already open in protest. But he shut it fast. His father was wearing The Look— times two. With a bitter taste in his mouth, Thomas stomped toward the sideboard and collected the balls. He plopped them onto the table and made for the door. Again, a firm hand planted itself on his shoulder.

"I believe I instructed you to give them to Master Alexander," Papa said.

Thomas could taste the bitterness again as he put both hands on the row of balls and shoved them across the table toward Alexander. He caught them nicely, and their eyes met. Alexander's had an odd look to them, as if he were fascinated by the whole scene.

"There," Thomas said roughly. He wanted to say, "You can't handle me any better than Clayton can. I suspect I won't be seeing you again." But one glance at his father's tight mouth and he settled for "Good-bye."

Thomas's mouth tasted so bitter by the time he left the room that he wanted to spit—preferably *on* someone. He slammed his bedroom door behind him and hurled himself onto the lumpy bed.

Surely Papa wouldn't keep this teacher, no matter how "interesting" he found Alexander's methods to be. They didn't work with Thomas, and that was all that mattered.

Nothing is going to work, Thomas thought. *So why waste Papa's money on someone who is just there to show how dumb I really am?*

That thought caught Thomas in a strange place, a place inside himself where he didn't go often. It was the place where tears and hurt feelings were kept. He pressed on his eyes to keep the tears from coming, but they seeped through his fingers. He wiped at them angrily.

"Please," he said out loud, "make Papa send Alexander away. Make him decide I don't have to do lessons at all. And don't let me cry!"

But whoever it was he was talking to wasn't listening this time, because Thomas put his face in his clumpy pillow and sobbed until he fell asleep.

Later, he woke to the sound of a bell tinkling in his ear. He rolled over to discover it was his mother's voice.

"Thomas," she said in her soft little way. "Wake up, son."

Thomas pulled himself up on his elbow and squinted at her in the gathering darkness.

"Is it night?" he said.

"No, there's just a storm brewing." She gave her chime-like laugh. "Two storms. One outside—and one downstairs in your father's study."

Thomas winced. "Is it about me?"

"I'm afraid so."

Mama passed her pale hand across his forehead, brushing back the wayward wisps of dark hair. Thomas sank back against the pillow.

"He's going to tell me my punishment," he said.

"Oh, no, Thomas, I don't think he plans to punish you. He only wants to tell you what he has decided."

Thomas set his jaw. "I don't want to know."

Mama laughed. "If it were up to me, I would scurry down the stairs and tell him that very thing. But you see, I think your father is right when he says I have spoiled you." She stood up. "Come on, then. I must do as Papa says and get you to the study."

"Do you always do everything Papa says?" Thomas asked.

"Yes, I do," she said.

Thomas screwed his face into a knot. "I know, because he's the head of our family."

"No," Mama said.

Thomas looked at her in surprise. Her voice was unusually sure.

"Because that is what God would have me do," she said.

"And I thank Him that John Hutchinson is a man who also does what God desires."

"God?" Thomas said. "How do you know . . . ?"

But Mama took his hand and led him to the door. "Not now, Thomas. Come on, then. Your father is waiting."

Papa was standing at the window when Thomas arrived, looking like the silhouette of a giant judge ready to hand down a sentence.

"Will you sit, Thomas?" his father said.

Thomas sank into a straight-backed chair and held on tightly to its green checked cloth seat.

"I will mince no words with you, Thomas," he said. "I was appalled by your behavior this morning with Master Alexander."

Thomas didn't have to ask what appalled meant. The disappointment was smeared all over Papa's face. Still, it might be worth it if it meant that teacher wouldn't be back.

"But it showed me," his father went on, "that there is more to be done with you than I thought. So . . . "

Thomas tried not to let his face brighten too much. *I'm going home!* he thought. *Papa is sending me home!*

"I have decided two things. One, I like this young teacher. He will stay on." Papa directed The Look at Thomas. "And there will be no more displays such as the one I saw today. Two—"

Thomas's heart had already sunk to the pit of his chest. He didn't see how the next piece of news could make him feel worse.

"I have arranged for you to spend five afternoons a week working as an assistant to Francis Pickering. He is the apothecary."

This time Thomas's heart flew to his throat, and he could

barely get out the words, "I'm to be an *apprentice?*"

"There is no shame in that," John Hutchinson said. "Benjamin Franklin himself was an apprentice to a printer. I think you can learn a great deal from Francis Pickering. He is honest and hard-working, and he doesn't know what it is to have everything handed to him."

"But I don't know anything about medicines!" Thomas cried.

"You'll learn soon enough, I'll warrant you."

Thomas had to hook his feet around the chair legs to keep himself from flying at his father. "But why?" he said. "I'm a Hutchinson. If I'm to inherit land and be a country gentleman, why must I learn a trade?"

His father shook his gold and silver head. "I can no longer promise you that that will happen," he said. "Everything is changing. It is sure that every man will have to earn his own way in this new nation."

He put his big hand on Thomas's shoulder and pulled him up. "But we can discuss that another time. You'll report to Francis Pickering at the apothecary shop on the Duke of Gloucester Street Monday afternoon after dinner."

"But—"

Papa tugged at his vest.

Thomas left the room with every hair on his neck standing straight up in anger.

Thomas was still brooding when he climbed out of bed the next morning. It was Sunday so there were no lessons, but he couldn't even be happy about that. Sitting in a damp, chilly pew between Papa and Clayton was only going to make things worse.

Mama, of course, was delighted with Bruton Parish Church, especially because the congregation didn't observe the custom of women sitting on one side of the church and men on the other.

The Hutchinsons sat in a pew near the front on the north side, because Papa was a vestryman of the church, which Clayton had told Thomas a hundred times was a very important thing to be. Thomas craned his neck to look up in the back gallery where the students sat to see if he could find Sam.

Clayton poked him. "Turn around, Thomas!" he hissed. "It isn't polite to gape about in church!"

Thomas crossed his arms sulkily over his chest. There wasn't that much to see anyway, he told himself. A stone floor. White walls that reminded him of air. Candles in globes on the walls that didn't have to be lit because the sun sizzled against the windows. Doors on each pew that a child shorter than he was wouldn't be able to see over. Red cushions to sit on, though the seat went up so straight that it felt like he had a ramrod up his back.

In spite of himself, Thomas noticed that the whole church was shaped like a cross, with a gallery on either side to form the cross part. The slaves and indentured servants sat in the left gallery, the college professors in the right. The altar was at the top of the cross, but it was too far away to be interesting.

Thomas squirmed. It had to be time to begin. Why didn't they start and get this over with? And where was everyone? The Hutchinsons seemed to be the only people sitting in their section.

Suddenly there was rustling from the back of the church, and Thomas sneaked a quick glance back before Clayton caught him. A bulky man with a long cape and poke holes for eyes was sailing up the aisle, and Thomas started to stand up.

"What are you doing?" Clayton whispered harshly. "That isn't the minister!"

"Who is it?" Thomas whispered back.

"It's Xavier Wormeley, one of the magistrates. He likes to make a grand entrance."

Thomas stared at the man as he swept grandly into his pew in front of them. His cheeks hung down on either side of his face and flopped like a turkey's neck. *Jowls*, Thomas was sure they were called.

Then there was another bit of rustling and an entire body of men and women in silk and lace ruffles floated in and took their places in the pews around the Hutchinsons. Clayton sniffed in disgust.

Thomas recognized most of the men, because he'd seen them at the Homestead from time to time. They were all plantation owners.

"Why did they come in like that?" Thomas whispered.

Clayton only glared at him, but Papa leaned his face in and said, "They come to church to be seen by the ordinary people."

Thomas didn't have time to ask any more questions because the organ began to blare and the service started. Within minutes, he didn't care anyway. There was a hymn that droned on under the fingers of Peter Pelham, the organist—whom Clayton had informed him was also the jailer—and reading from the *Book of Common Prayer* and a long sermon by Reverend Edmund Pendleton from high up in his pulpit. The only thing that kept Thomas awake was that he knew he would see Sam after the service.

His brother was standing with his school friends out in

the churchyard when Thomas came out, and he was ready to shout, "Sam! Over here!"

But Sam put his arm around the shoulders of another boy and punched him playfully. The other boy caught Sam's head in the crook of his arm, and they all laughed. As he watched, a pang went through Thomas.

Ever since he'd been in Williamsburg, he hadn't played at all. There was no one to chase or punch—or even splash in a brook with or play tag or ball with. He was surrounded by people on the steps of the church, but he had never felt more alone.

Sam spotted him then, and he smiled a dazzling smile and waved. Before Thomas could run to him, he jabbed one of his schoolmates lightly in the ribs and then took off running down the Duke of Gloucester Street with the whole group in pursuit. Thomas watched until they disappeared into the college.

"Come along home now, Thomas," Mama said at his elbow. "Papa is going to have dinner at the Raleigh with the other vestrymen." She squeezed his arm warmly. "You'll need to rest. You have a big day coming up tomorrow."

Thomas set his jaw. A big day? It was going to be a terrible day. And there wasn't even a friend to tell that to.

✛ ⚜ ✛

Chapter Six

Thomas woke up the next morning with a decision in his head. He would go to lessons with Master Alexander, and he would report for work to Francis Pickering in the apothecary shop. But he wouldn't try. He would be as unpleasant as he could be. If he kept that up, very soon they would give up on him, and Papa would be ashamed enough to send him back to the plantation where he belonged.

Thomas climbed out of bed to put on his working clothes—a pair of buckskin breeches and a shirt made of an itchy fabric that Esther called Virginia cloth.

It's a good plan, he told himself firmly.

There was a thin drizzle falling as Thomas crossed from the back of the house to the kitchen building, and he was anxious to get inside by the brick fireplace that was big enough for him to stand up in.

But there was a chill inside, and it came from Esther. Her bones were aching with the damp weather, and her humor matched it.

"Where have you been, child?" she barked. "I've had to poke the fire myself, and I'm in no condition for it this morning. Not with a roof that leaks on me every step of the way." She stopped and shook a fist at the beams in the kitchen ceiling.

"It's unfit to shelter a *dog* a gentleman had regard for!"

Thomas grunted and picked up a small barrel by its metal handle and headed toward the door. The next thing he knew, he was sprawled on the floor, watching the bucket bounce crazily toward the wall.

"Have you tripped over your own feet again?" Esther said.

"No!" Thomas said. He scowled at her as he gathered himself up from the floor. "There's a loose board there. Otis ought to fix that!"

"And *you* ought to watch where you're a-goin'!" Esther said. "Although if that happens, I will give my head for a football."

She continued to mutter about Otis being too old to be repairing floors and herself being too old to be cooking for her master's family.

And I shouldn't be fetching water either, Thomas added as he strode, red-faced, toward the well with the barrel.

The well was shared by several households, but so far, Thomas hadn't run into anyone else there when he went to get water. Esther had informed him that that was because he "laid a'bed too long in the mornin's and everyone else got there ahead of him."

But today, he saw a girl about his age just about to slide the rope through her barrel handle.

"You there!" he called to her. "Have you any business using this well?"

"I have as much right to be here as you have," she said. "Perhaps more. Who are you, anyway?"

Thomas just gawked at her. He had never had many dealings with girls, other than the squawking ones at the Homestead who scattered like sparrows whenever he was around. It was pretty certain this girl wasn't planning to scatter *or* squawk. Not yet, anyway.

She looked calmly at him now with a pair of perfectly round brown eyes that seemed to take up most of the top half of her face. She had a mouth shaped like a slice of melon, and her teeth were white and shiny.

"Well?" she said again. "Who are you?"

"Who are *you?*" Thomas said, setting down his barrel and taking one menacing step forward.

"I asked you first."

"But I'm of a better sort, and you are a servant. Therefore, I ask the questions."

The melon-slice mouth broke into a grin that seemed to dimple her cheeks in 20 places. "If you are of a better sort," she said, "why are you fetching water?"

Thomas stopped with his mouth half open and tried not to *look* as if he were searching helplessly for an answer.

"Never mind that," he said. "Just answer my question."

"No," she said. "I'll tell you nothing."

Thomas squared his jaw. "Fine. I don't really want to know anyway. Just get out of the way so I can get my water."

"As soon as I've got mine," she said.

"I don't think so," Thomas said. He pushed up his sleeves and went straight for the well. "You must let me go first because I—"

"I know, I know," said the girl, "because you are of a better sort." She sniffed and jumped down from the well, pulling the barrel behind her. "It doesn't seem so to me, but what am I to do when faced with a bully such as yourself?"

Thomas stopped and glared at her. "Bully? What's a bully?"

She took off her mob cap and shook out a head full of straight, silky hair the color of sand. "A bully is someone who enjoys making other people do what he wants them to do just because he's bigger than they are. You could pick me up and throw me down the well," she said, "and there's nothing I can do about it, so please, go first."

Thomas knew he should have felt like the conqueror as he jumped up on the well's edge and clumsily fastened the rope to his barrel. But something about this victory made him feel like he'd just lost.

Putting hand over hand as fast as he could, Thomas lowered the barrel into the well. He was careful to keep a mean scowl on his face, because the brown-eyed girl was watching him.

He peered down into the well and saw the water rising to the barrel's brim. It was time to puff out his chest and make this girl understand that it was only right that someone so *powerful* should go first. He pulled up the rope hard and fast, and the barrel rose as lightly as if it had been empty.

Because it was—or nearly so. As the barrel emerged above the top of the well, the last of the water poured from the bottom and left the container swinging vacantly.

Thomas heard a shout of laughter coming from the girl. He snatched the barrel into his hands and roughly turned it over. The bottom was cracked, and two of the side slats were split wide open. It must have happened when he'd dropped it in the kitchen.

He hurled the barrel across the grass and dove off the side of the well, rolling only long enough to catch himself and scramble to his feet. The girl was still howling as he ran toward home. And there wasn't a whisper of fear in her voice.

Once he'd confessed to breaking the barrel to Esther, a trip to the cooper's shop to have it mended was added to Thomas's already long list of chores.

"You can do that on the way to the apothecary's this afternoon," she told him.

Thomas groaned to himself. He'd almost forgotten about that. And there was little time to think about it now, with the table to clear, the walkways to sweep, the cooking fire to be constantly stoked, and the chickens to feed.

What happened to the days when Esther was taking orders from me? Thomas groused to himself. He was more determined than ever to be sent back to the plantation, where perhaps everyone would remember how he was supposed to be treated.

Alexander was already in the dining room with his bulging book satchel when Thomas arrived for lessons later.

"Please, Thomas, have a seat," he said gaily.

"No," Thomas said.

"Very well, then, stand if you like. I prefer to sit."

Thomas stood like a post at the table's edge while Alexander pushed a chair back and lounged in it.

"I learned quite a bit about you last time," he said.

"I am not interested," Thomas said.

"What are you interested in?"

"Nothing."

"You lie!"

"I do not!"

"You are interested in two things that I know of. One, convincing your father to run me out on the high road. And two, bedeviling other children."

"How do you know?" Thomas demanded.

Alexander looked suspiciously around the room and then leaned forward so intently that Thomas couldn't keep himself from leaning in, too.

"I have spies," Alexander whispered.

Thomas snorted loudly and stood up straight again. "*You* lie!"

"You don't know that, my boy. Remember, appearances can be deceiving."

Thomas folded his arms and said nothing.

"Tell me, Thomas, do you know what a spy is?"

"Yes, of course I do."

"What is it?"

"I don't . . . I'm not going to say."

"Because you don't know." Alexander cocked his head to one side. "I took you for a shrewd young man who knows how to get his way, and I thought you something of a bully, but I never would have thought you were a coward."

That was the second time today Thomas had heard the new word *bully*. But it was the other word—*coward*—that captured him.

"I am not a coward! I'm brave enough to take you on right now!"

Thomas went for the buttons on his vest, but Alexander put up his hand.

"Whether or not you can beat me to a pulp in a fight has nothing to do with your being a coward or not. A coward is someone who is afraid to admit that he is wrong, or that he doesn't know something."

"Someone who doesn't know something is stupid!"

"Does your father know all the military secrets of the British Royal Navy?"

"No!"

"He's stupid, then."

Thomas pressed his hands on the table. "Never call my father stupid!"

"I didn't. You did."

Thomas looked around for something to throw at Alexander. He picked up a book, and Alexander let out one of his cheers.

"I'm so glad you've selected that one. It's my own personal favorite. Come, read aloud to me."

Thomas looked at the volume he'd grabbed and tried to decipher the title. A chill went up his spine. He could read almost anything that Clayton had ever put in front of him, although he had never let Clayton know that. But this was a word he had never seen before.

The Aeneid? What does that mean?

"I don't want to," Thomas said.

"Coward."

Thomas slammed the book on the table. "Say that one more time—"

"Admit it! You don't know that word. Why would you? It's Latin!"

Thomas didn't answer, but shoved *The Aeneid* away. Alexander caught it in its slide and opened it up.

"As you wish. I shall read aloud."

He began to read, and Thomas thought of putting his fingers in his ears. But something told him Alexander would find a way to make that a part of the lesson, too.

Noisily, Thomas scraped a chair to the other corner of the room and sat in it. There was no possible way this day could get any worse, he thought.

But he was wrong.

✢ ✢ ✢

Chapter Seven

*A*lexander read until they heard the bell ring for dinner. Thomas jumped at the sound. The time had fled by, because he had been working hard not to get pulled in by the adventure Alexander was spinning out, about some man from Troy whose mother was a Greek goddess and who was wandering all over the world in search of—

It isn't worth remembering, Thomas told himself quickly. *Stupid story. Stupider teacher.*

"Excellent start!" Alexander sang out as he collected his books and his dimples and prepared to leave. "Now that you have the idea of the story, tomorrow you can read to me."

Thomas grunted.

"I shall regard that as a yes," Alexander said.

The table was set for dinner in the front parlor. With the fire crackling in the fireplace, it was a cheery room, even with the sky a slate-gray outside. But Thomas felt anything but cheery. Esther's dinner was meat pie that wasn't quite cooked all the way and hoe cake that coated his tongue like sawdust.

"I think Esther's cooking is improving somewhat, don't you, sir?" Virginia Hutchinson said to her husband.

Thomas smothered a snort and looked at his father. Father just cocked a bushy eyebrow and cleared his throat.

"Well, then, Thomas, what did you learn at lessons today?"

Thomas choked on a mouthful of crumbs. "No one told me I had to report—"

"I am telling you now. Come on, then, what was it? More ball games?"

At first, Thomas groped, but then he had an idea—for shaming Alexander.

"I learned that there is more than one god," Thomas said. "And that some of them are women."

Papa's fork clattered to his plate, and Mama dabbed nervously at her mouth with a napkin.

"What's this?" John Hutchinson asked.

"One of the female gods—that would be a goddess, I suppose—was the mother of A—" Thomas's thoughts scrambled. "A-nee-us. A Greek poet wrote a poem about him because he was a hero." Thomas cocked his head slyly. "I thought you had always talked of only one God, but I suppose I was mistaken. There must be a dozen or more!"

There was a shocked silence at the table, and Thomas happily wrapped his fingers around the handle of the silver porringer he was eating from. Even the meat pie tasted better, now that Master Alexander was practically unemployed.

And then his father put his hands on the table, leaned his face toward his plate, and laughed—so hard his hoe cake bounced onto the table linen.

Mama giggled anxiously, while Thomas stared.

"What is it, John?" she said.

"'Tis mythology, that's what it is!" Papa roared merrily.

"Myth—what? What is that?"

Papa wiped mirthful tears away from his eyes and chuckled

as he spoke. "The ancient Greeks made up stories about an entire regiment of gods and goddesses to explain the things they didn't understand, like why the sun comes up and why there are seasons. Those stories are called mythology." Papa put his hands on his stomach and chortled again. "It's none of it true, of course, but some of the poems are works of great classic literature that every educated man should be familiar with. A good choice on Master Alexander's part."

Mama's laugh rang lightly over the table. Thomas, on the other hand, wanted to dump the contents of his porringer onto the floor.

"I'm so relieved!" Mama said. "I thought for a moment our handsome young schoolmaster was teaching Thomas some heathen religion!"

"Well, I know this for certain," John Hutchinson said, taking care of the last of the laughing tears. "I must attend to your religious education, son, or you shall swallow whatever story you are fed. And that is a serious matter."

But after one somber moment, Papa burst into laughter again and Mama with him.

Thomas angrily pushed his uneaten pork around in the dish with his fork. *Isn't there any way I can drive this scoundrel out of my life?* he thought.

After dinner, Esther told Thomas that the cooper's shop, where he was to take the barrel for repair, was in the mill yard. As he walked toward it across mucky North England Street, he heard a burst of noise at the other end of the street. He stopped and craned his neck to see, and as he did, a gang of boys exploded from the yard and into the street, straight toward him.

"Yer lousy rebels, and we'll see you hanged for sure!" one boy shouted from the back of the pack.

"You'll have to catch us first, Tory!" cried another in the front, and as if to prove it he tore down the road with his companions roaring right behind him, and the "Tories" pounding the mud behind them. They were headed straight for Thomas.

He clutched the handle of the barrel and dove for the side, barely missing being trampled by the lot of them. But as he rolled onto the wooden walkway, he felt something warm and wet and heavy splat against the side of his face, and another one splatter squarely in the middle of his back.

Thomas put his fingers to his face and brought back a handful of thick, oozy mud. He could feel his eyes blazing as he looked up at the mob of boys. They had stopped in the middle of North England Street and were facing each other in two lines, pelting one another with the biggest balls of goop they could scoop up from the muddy road.

"Hey, you there!" Thomas cried out. "How dare you?"

Most of the boys ignored him and kept on volleying mudballs. But one boy noticed him and dodged several missiles to get to him. He stood over Thomas with his arms crossed, wearing a rag wrapped around his head and a cloth half-mask with only the eyes cut out.

He thinks that mask scares me, Thomas thought as he scrambled to his feet. *But he's only about half my size. I can take him in an instant.*

"Traitor or Loyalist?" the boy asked.

"What?"

"Are you a traitor to King George of England who by rights rules this land—or are you loyal to him and his government?"

Thomas shoved back the sleeves of his homespun shirt, mud slopping through the folds.

"I'm a Patriot!" Thomas declared.

"Oh," the boy said. He jerked a small thumb toward one side of the battle going on behind him. "Then you're with them. But you have to be a Tory next time."

Thomas stared at him. "I don't ever want to be a Tory!"

"But we have to take turns." Then the boy grinned, revealing a slice of a smile and a row of big white teeth.

He must be the brother of that girl I saw at the well this morning, Thomas thought. *The one who laughed at me.*

Thomas doubled up his fists. "Have you a sister?"

But the boy just grinned again and slipped back into the game. Thomas started after him, but the mud sliding down his face stopped him. It was probably better not to get any more dirt on him before he went to the apothecary's. He would take care of this fellow next time.

Thomas wiped his sleeve on his breeches and carried the barrel to the mill yard.

By the time he had left the barrel for repair, the boys were long gone from the street, and Thomas hurried on, his thoughts hurrying with him.

And I'm not interested in another tongue lashing from my father. I'd best get to the apothecary's. Although come to think of it, he might not want me to work for him if I'm in the habit of being late.

But once more Thomas's ponderings were brought to a sudden halt, this time by something above him—something that moved.

Thomas slowed his steps and looked up at the house he was passing, just behind the mill, on the corner of North

England and Nicholson Streets. He thought he'd seen something at one of the windows. Something white and flowing. . . .

Thomas's mouth fell open. The white hadn't been a bird at all. It had been a lacy apron, worn by a girl who was looking down at him. Even from here he could see the perfectly round eyes, slice-of-melon smile, and big white teeth.

It was the girl he'd seen at the well. And she was still laughing at him.

"Who *are* you?" Thomas shouted up at her.

But she only put her hand in front of her mouth and jumped away from the window. Thomas clenched his teeth together. He had never fought a female, but he might make an exception in the case of this little servant girl.

Not now, though. There was the apothecary's to get to.

Thomas tore across the lot behind Chowning's Tavern and took Queen Street to the Duke of Gloucester Street at a dead run. His father had told him the shop was almost at the end of this main road, just before the Capitol Building. He was snorting like a bull by the time he reached it, and he stopped in front to catch his breath.

Pickering's Apothecary was a two-story narrow gray building with two shop windows downstairs and two shuttered ones above. Between the second-story windows was the usual sign hanging from a pole. This one had a painting of a jar with a stick coming out of it.

All the shops had pictures on their signs. Clayton had told him that those signs—the shoe on the shoemaker's, the wig for the barber's, a pig for the pork vendor's—were for people who couldn't read, and he would be one of them if he didn't attend to his lessons.

Thomas took one more swipe at his muddy shirt and went up the two steps and in the tall, black door. As soon as he opened it, his nose was filled with the scents of ginger and cloves. But he stopped inside the doorway and gaped.

There in front of him were cabinet after green cabinet lining the walls, with shelf upon shelf of jars, bottles, and little drawers. Each one bore a label edged in gold gilt, and their black letters screamed out things like:

ICHLHYOCOLLA
RAD:IPEEACUAN
VIN:TECTIF:CONG
CHALY: OF SULPH

Thomas knew he must have gasped, because a wide man standing at the counter turned to look at him. Thomas stared at the man's flapping jowls. It was Xavier Wormeley, the magistrate.

"Is this the boy you've been waiting for, Francis?" Magistrate Wormeley asked.

Thomas froze.

From behind the counter, a voice wheezed out, "Young Hutchinson! Where have you been? I better hear a good story, or you are in a world of trouble!"

⁜ ⁃✚⁃ ⁜

Chapter Eight

Thomas turned slowly.

Another man with beady eyes peered at Thomas out of a pair of gold-rimmed spectacles, and his head seemed to barely reach above the shiny wood-topped counter.

He wasted no time in darting out on a pair of spindly legs that were wrapped tight in black wool stockings. The little wrinkled man must have been upward of 60, Thomas thought, but he moved like a bird who had something after him.

This must be Francis Pickering.

He skittered right up to Thomas and pointed a long, slender finger directly at his face.

"You are late," he said, his voice high-pitched and wheezing. "That will not be accepted from here on." His dark bird eyes scanned Thomas swiftly. "And you're not to show up looking as if you slept with the pigs. You didn't, did you?"

Thomas numbly shook his head. Everything was happening so fast that he couldn't get his lips to make words.

Old Francis waved his hand impatiently and started back to the counter. "Go out to the east yard. There's water in a barrel. Wash yourself up while I get Mr. Wormeley's cinnamon oil. You say the pain is worse?"

"What?" Thomas asked.

61

"Not you. You go and wash, and see you don't touch any-thing between here and there. Never touch anything until I've told you to. Do you understand?"

You don't have to tell me that, Thomas thought miser-ably as he made his way down a dark hallway and out a side door. *I don't want to touch any of your old bottles anyway.*

While he scooped handfuls of water out of the barrel and splashed them on his face and arms, Thomas looked around. He was all the way at the end of town. Surely there must be a runaway route from here.

He craned his neck to see around the Capitol Building. There was almost nothing behind it except that one house with the—

Oh, Thomas thought. *That's the jail.*

His shoulders sagged as he trudged back inside the side door. Francis was still seeing the bulging magistrate off, so Thomas dallied in the dark hallway and looked around.

On his right there were two sets of steps, one curving up and disappearing into the second story, and one leading straight down into a pit as black as night. Ahead was the room he had passed when he left the shop to go outside, and Thomas stretched to see into it.

It was a stark white room with blue trim for the chair rail and around the windows. In the center sat a desk with a quill pen propped in an inkwell and books flopped open to what looked like more of the scribbles Thomas had seen on the bottles and jars. Thomas could feel his mouth going dry.

But when his eyes lit on the object in the corner, his lips parted into a gaping hole. There, between the two windows, hanging limply on a stand, was a skeleton. And there was no mistaking it—it was the skeleton of a human being.

Thomas's thoughts began to chase around, untamed, in his head. *I'm to work here? Where this humpbacked old man studies the dead bodies of humans? There's no telling what he has down in the cellar! Is that where he . . . does it?*

"What are you about there, boy?" Francis rasped from the shop. "Come on, then. There's work to be done!"

Thomas peeled his eyes away from the bony figure in the corner and hurried into the shop. Mr. Wormeley had gone, and Francis was tapping his fingers impatiently on the countertop. Thomas knew there was no time to play games as he was doing with Master Alexander.

"Master Francis," Thomas said. "I must tell you, you don't want me working here. I—"

"You're right about that," Francis said. "I need an apprentice, not some infant I'm going to have to raise." He took another gasping breath. "I want a young man I can trust to live upstairs and keep his eye out at night for thieves. But you're too young to do that job, though I must say you're a strapping big boy for 10."

He stopped to wheeze in more air.

"No, I *don't* want you working here. But I would do anything for John Hutchinson and, I regret to say, that includes taking on his son as an assistant. But mind you—"

The long finger came out again and pointed toward Thomas's nose. "I expect you to work. Don't give me any of your gentry airs just because you think I'm an ordinary sort. Your father has never treated me as such and neither will you."

Francis darted out from behind the counter and began directing his finger at items in the shop so fast that Thomas found himself always three things behind.

"You will learn to compound medicines," the old man

said. "You'll search the woods for the plants I need, you will keep things neat and tidy, and you will assist me at treatments. You'll run your legs to the bone delivering medicines—"

That's what happened to his last apprentice, Thomas thought crazily. *He was run to the bone, and that's him hanging up in the office!*

"—if you've a mind for it, you'll learn to keep the books, too, and collect fees. Patients will sometimes take upward of six months to pay their bills. Now, I will accept wood, hay, and oats as payment—" Francis suddenly stopped and shook his head. "Though nothing milled by that Loyalist. But we shall get to that later. Now . . . "

Thomas's head was spinning, and it only turned faster as Francis went on circling the shop, poking at this, and picking up that, and waving it before Thomas's terrified eyes.

"That is the examination room back there," Francis said, jabbing a thumb toward the Skeleton Room. "Down in the cellar is the laboratory where the medicines are mixed. This is the shop where they are sold. Now, we sell no patent medicines made by those wretched English. No, sir, we have plenty of medicines made right here in Virginia. I've found 21 medicinal plants native to this colony to date—and you, boy, will learn them all."

Thomas's own breathing was starting to drown out Francis's voice, but it didn't matter. He wasn't understanding a thing the old man was saying anyway. It was all a jumble of words like *elixirs and ointments*.

Some of the materials were stored in black bottles so the sun couldn't filter through and evaporate them, and other things were held in the blue and white jars. There were pill, ointment, and syrup pots. There were frightening-looking surgical instruments in velvet-lined cases whose names slid in and out of Thomas's head like sand on the loose.

By the time Francis had finished his lecture, Thomas had only remembered one thing. And he recalled that only because Francis had gotten so close to Thomas's face that Thomas could smell licorice on the old man's wheezing breath.

First the apothecary pulled a chain from around his waist and showed Thomas a key attached to it, which he used to unlock a glass-doored cabinet behind the counter. He took out a dark-brown jar that had no label and held it in his hands as if it were some sacred vessel.

"This is gold powder," he said solemnly. "From real gold." He paused, as if waiting for Thomas to gasp, and then went on. "As you know, gold and other precious metals have healing power. I coat all my pills with gold powder to speed up the cure."

This was where Francis, still cradling the jar, brought his face close to Thomas's and said, "There is great wealth in this jar and the others like it in the cellar. See that you guard them with your life. You have no idea what I will do to you if any harm comes to it at your hands."

Thomas didn't know whether to nod, shake his head, or dash for the door. Francis didn't give him a chance to do any of them. He set down the jar and thrust a broom into his hand and said, "Go down to the laboratory and sweep. Every nook and cranny, mind you! I keep a spotless shop at all times."

With heavy steps, Thomas headed for the stairs. He tried not to look at the skeleton as he went by.

It was so dark that Thomas had to feel his way down to the cellar. When he reached the bottom, something brushed across the top of his head and he screamed and ducked, letting go of the broom handle as he dove for the floor. His hands flew over his head, and he lay there shaking.

Any minute now—any second—it's going to reach down and grab me! Thomas whimpered to himself. *Please, please, don't let me die here in this miserable cellar!*

He lay there shaking for a moment . . . but still nothing happened. Thomas peeked out from under his arms and made out a long table and several cabinets with more of the same bottles and jars like he'd seen in the shop. One had a lock like the cabinet with the gold jar in it upstairs. Holding his breath, Thomas dared a glance upward. There they were—the things!—hanging, swaying from the ceiling!

Were those . . . they must be the . . . remains of . . . patients . . . apprentices . . . waiting to become skeletons!

A final chill ran through Thomas, and he tore madly for the stairs. Something caught on the toe of his boot, and with one giant sprawl he was back on the floor. He crawled like a frightened crab to the steps. Suddenly, light flickered on the walls of the stairwell, and Thomas shot his terrified eyes toward it.

Standing at the top of the steps was Francis Pickering, candlelight playing wickedly across his face.

"What in the name of Beelzebub is going on down there?"

"Oh, nothing, sir!" Thomas managed to get out.

"Well, 'nothing' surely makes a good deal of racket. Have you done with the sweeping?"

"Not quite. I—"

"Never mind. I need for you to make a delivery, and then there's the shop to be swept. . . ."

Thomas kept saying "Yes, sir," and as soon as Francis disappeared from the doorway, he groped for the broom and tore up the steps. *I'll do anything he says*, Thomas thought, *just don't let him turn me into a skeleton.*

By the time Thomas stumbled wearily home in the gathering dimness of that evening, he was convinced that none of his father's servants worked as hard as he had that day—and all with old Francis squinting at him over his spectacles.

Thomas had been wrapping medicines in newspaper and tying them with twine to be delivered when he'd dropped a whole vial of ginger syrup meant for Mistress Prentiss's cough and smashed it into a hundred pieces. Francis had squinted.

Thomas had been delivering ginseng for Mr. Wetherburn's fatigue in a package—neatly wrapped and addressed in Francis's perfect handwriting—when he had accidentally stepped on Mistress Wetherburn's tulips. She had followed him all the way back to the apothecary shop and shouted about Thomas's clumsiness in front of three customers. Old Francis had just squinted at Thomas.

Thomas had stood next to the apothecary, who was holding the Epsom salts while he drew a splinter out of little Will Hayes's foot. When Francis picked up a tiny, sharp-pointed instrument, Thomas had all but fainted and had to go outside for air. He could feel old Francis squinting after him.

If Francis Pickering went to his father tomorrow morning and told him he didn't want Thomas working for him, that would be the best thing he could ever wish for. But it was clear to Thomas that old Francis didn't work that way.

If he wants to be rid of me, Thomas thought, heart pounding, *he will just . . . get rid of me . . . for good!*

✝ ✝ ✝

Chapter Nine

"Hutchinson! You there, young Hutchinson! Where is that gold leaf I asked you for?"

Thomas's eyes sprang open. Had it been only a dream or had he really heard old Francis screaming at him?

He pulled his head up and rubbed his forehead. Below him was the counter, now bearing a puddle of his drool. Thomas hurriedly mopped it up with the apron Francis had given him to wear and looked frantically toward the examination room door.

"Where is that gold leaf?" came the wheezing shout. "I have a tooth waiting here!"

Thomas scrambled to the drawer behind the counter where the gold and silver leaves were kept and snatched up a handful. Half of it spilled on the floor as he tripped on the threshold going into the exam room.

Francis squinted at it over his spectacles, and Thomas saw his forehead go red, all the way up to the top of his head where his gray hair started. He'd noticed in these past two weeks that whenever Francis was exceptionally annoyed with him, his scalp turned a brilliant scarlet.

"Sorry, sir," Thomas muttered.

"Just give me the leaf you've managed to hold on to so I can pack this tooth."

Thomas handed it over and watched as Francis rolled it into a ball and stuffed it into the tooth of Mistress Wetherburn. She rolled her bulging eyes first at Thomas, then back at Francis.

"Get back into the shop, boy," Francis said to him. "You're upsetting the patient."

Even with her mouth wide open, Mistress Wetherburn managed to get out something about the trampling of her tulips. Thomas backed gratefully out of the room . . . and straight into someone.

"Look where yer goin' there, boy!" said a voice that sounded like heels on pebbles.

Thomas spun around and looked up at a tall man. His eyes went through Thomas like a pair of musket balls.

"Can I help you?" Thomas asked, scooting behind the counter.

"I need some cloves," the man said.

"Ground or whole?"

"Whole, of course," the man said. "It's for my son's toothache."

He jerked his head to one side, and for the first time, Thomas realized there was a boy about his own age with the man.

He was taller than Thomas, but skinny as a bamboo stalk, and Thomas could tell from the paper-thin homespun shirt that hung limply from his narrow shoulders that he was of a lower class than himself. He didn't appear to be anyone's servant, though, for there was an I-dare-you look on his face no servant would have thought to put on.

Even now, he narrowed his dull eyes at Thomas, who glared back at him and went for the clove jar.

"How many?" he asked the man.

"One. Give me one."

Thomas set the jar on the counter and looked directly into the boy's face. *You aren't so tough*, he let his eyes tell him.

"You can use this two ways," Thomas said. "Either bite down on it, or squeeze out the oil and rub it on your tooth."

"Henry ain't stupid," the man said. "He's had a rotten tooth before."

Thomas couldn't hold back a smile. "I'm sure he has."

"What does that mean?" the boy said.

In spite of himself, Thomas drew back a little. With his lips so thin and colorless, the boy's mouth had been nothing more than a slit until now. When he spoke, it was as if his face had come open like an ugly gash.

"Hutchinson!" said the wheezy voice from the doorway. "Has this man paid you yet?"

"Not yet, sir," Thomas said. "We were just getting to that."

"Well, get to it quickly. Gates, you have no credit with me."

"I know, I know," said the man gruffly. "If there were another apothecary left in town, I'd go there."

"And a happy man I'd be," Francis said.

"That will be a half-pence," Thomas said, holding out his hand. He could barely keep a grin from sneaking onto his face. This wasn't such a bad business after all, not with being allowed to put the likes of this Gates fellow in his place.

Gates smashed a coin into Thomas's palm and turned to go, but Henry stood fast, staring Thomas down with his disturbing mouth gaping like a wound.

Thomas met his eyes without blinking and put the top back on the clove jar as he glared. But it was hard to do without looking and before he could stop it, the jar slipped from his hand and dumped 50 cloves across the counter.

Francis groaned and went back to the examination room. Gates continued out the door without so much as a backward glance. But Henry pulled his slit-mouth open even wider, and he laughed.

Thomas clenched the counter with both hands. "You're done with your business," he said to Henry through his teeth. "Why don't you go?"

"Because I hate to miss a good freak show," he said.

It was only because Francis at that moment rasped out "Hutchinson!" that Thomas didn't leap over the counter and take Henry down in the middle of the apothecary shop.

"Yes, sir!" he called back, and Henry sauntered loosely to the door with his long arms and legs dangling like a puppet's.

"I've made up some troches of licorice root and sugar for Elizabeth Tarpley's cough," Francis said from the doorway. "See that you deliver them to her store."

Gladly, Thomas thought as he dove under the counter across the room and grabbed the package he had wrapped earlier. *No scrawny puppet laughs at me and gets away with it.*

He tore up the Duke of Gloucester to the corner of Boutetourt Street and practically dumped the package into Elizabeth Tarpley's lap before dashing back out into the road to find Henry Gates.

Just as Thomas darted back out onto Duke of Gloucester, a man in a black hat with a wide brim rounded the corner on the other side and began to ring a bell he held in his hand.

"Hear ye, hear ye!" he cried out. "British General Clinton has crossed into Charleston, South Carolina, with 10,000 soldiers. American General Lincoln has only 5,000. Hear ye! Hear ye!"

The man continued on down the street, chanting his

message again, and heads began to poke out of shop doors and tavern windows.

That must be the town crier, Thomas thought. But right now, he was only interested in finding Henry Gates.

And just then, there he was, following his father up the wooden steps into Chowning's Tavern.

Just as I thought—a lower sort, Thomas thought. Members of the gentry, like his father, never ate at Chowning's but went instead to Wetherburn's or the Raleigh.

"You there!" Thomas shouted as he ran to the center of the wide, muddy avenue. "Henry Gates!"

The boy stopped on the steps and looked back at Thomas. He turned to watch his father go into the tavern and then ran toward Thomas, arms and legs dangling the whole way. Thomas crossed his arms over his chest and watched him.

Henry stopped a few feet away and put his bony hands on his hips. "What do you want?"

"I think you know."

Henry's mouth cut open. "Have you got your dander up because I laughed at you?"

Thomas took a step forward, but Henry didn't draw back.

"Big bumbling thing like you," Henry said, "and can't even put a jar lid on without spilling it."

"Take that back!" Thomas cried.

"Why should I?"

"Because I'm your better!"

"Oh, are you now? Since when is an apothecary's apprentice better than a leathersmith's son?"

"I'm no apprentice!" Thomas hissed, his cheeks burning and his fists doubling up. "I'm Thomas Hutchinson, a plantation owner's son!"

"Thomas Hutchinson?"

Henry narrowed his eyes, and then he turned his head and spat in the middle of the street. "Thomas Hutchinson was the Royal Governor of Massachusetts. The Patriots drove him out of Boston after the first battle, and he ran like a coward!"

Thomas brought both fists up in front of him. "I'm no relation to him!" he lashed out. "We Hutchinsons are Virginians and Patriots, through and through. And there's not a coward among us!"

With that he let fly with a punch that landed right on the side of Henry's surprised face.

Henry didn't wait for Thomas's next blow, but ran to one side, dodged Thomas's fist, and weaved the other way. He took off up Gloucester with Thomas thundering on his heels.

The scrawny Gates boy was fast, and Thomas didn't catch him until they were almost to the Raleigh Tavern. But Thomas was stronger and in an instant he had him pinned to the mud in the middle of the road and was sitting astride him.

"Get off," Henry cried.

"Not until you take it all back! Every word!"

Henry tightened his mouth, and Thomas pulled back his arm to give it the punch it deserved, when his wrist was caught by a hand even stronger than his own.

"Get up, Thomas Hutchinson!" someone said behind him. "Get off that boy at once, I say!"

Thomas didn't even have to look to see who was speaking. It was the deep, booming voice of his father.

As soon as Thomas was yanked to his feet, Henry scrambled up and disappeared behind the King's Arms Tavern.

"He's getting away!" Thomas yelled.

"Thank the Lord!" Papa said. "You could have killed that boy. He's half your weight!"

"He insulted the Hutchinson name!"

"And so did you, rolling around in the middle of the Duke of Gloucester Street like a common ruffian! Have you ever known me to put my fist into another man's face because he insulted me?"

Thomas shook his head.

"Then whatever possessed you?"

"He's of a lower sort than we are," Thomas said, drawing his shirtsleeve across his face. "I couldn't let him get away with it."

To Thomas's surprise, Papa put his hand on his shoulder. "You have no idea what this war we are fighting is really about, do you?"

"Independence from England," he said sulkily.

Papa gave Thomas a gentle push toward the apothecary shop and walked beside him.

"Independence from England is only one part of it. Our men are fighting for a very different life, Thomas. If we win this war, the lower classes will no longer be considered common wretches that crawl upon the earth. All men will be considered equal. No one will really be better than anyone else, and that is an equality such as no other nation has ever had before. And do you know where men like Thomas Jefferson got such an idea?"

"No, sir," Thomas said.

"From God." Papa smiled a little. "The one true God, not some father of Aeneas." The smile faded as they reached the front steps of the shop. Papa turned Thomas to face him and put both hands on his shoulders. "It is by a special providence that God is allowing the creation of this new nation. We must prepare ourselves for it. That is why I want you to have an education. That is why I want you to have practical skills as well. I want you to be simple and honest and well-meaning, as God intends, because only in that way will you be truly free."

He gave Thomas's shoulders a squeeze and let go. "And that does not include beating your peers to a pulp—in the street or anywhere else."

Thomas's head was spinning. He had always been told—by Clayton and Esther, and even Mama—that because they were the Hutchinsons, they could always expect to be treated with respect because they were somehow better than most people. Papa had just taken that idea and turned it completely upside down.

"Now that I have told you all of that," Papa said, "I am going to go back on some of it. I don't think it wise for you to hang about with the likes of young Gates there. Not because he is of a lower sort, but because he is of a rougher, more dishonest sort. I don't trust him."

"Francis doesn't trust him either," Thomas said.

"That's because Francis has a good head on those hunched-up shoulders of his! You pay attention, son. You will learn a great deal from that old curmudgeon."

"What's a 'curmudgeon'?"

A smile broke across Papa's face, for no reason that Thomas could think of. "A curmudgeon," he said, "is a bad-tempered person, though in this case he's one who wouldn't hurt so much as an ant. Why, the old man has spent his whole life making people well." Papa gave him a final pat. "You'd best get back to work now. I'll see you at supper time."

"Yes, sir," Thomas said vaguely as he went up the steps.

He still couldn't figure out why his question about the curmudgeon had made his father smile like that—in a way he'd never seen him grin before.

But there was no time to think about that now.

"Hutchinson!" the old curmudgeon cried. "Where have you been?"

And he didn't sound to Thomas like a man who wouldn't hurt an ant.

Chapter Ten

One morning before lessons, Esther sent Thomas to the cooper's to inquire after the barrel.

"He's had it upward of two weeks," she grumbled, shaking a wooden spoon at Thomas as if he alone were responsible for the cooper's tardiness.

Thomas took his time strolling toward the miller's yard. It was a soft April morning, and the streets seemed to have come alive in the time Thomas had been in Williamsburg.

The naked dogwood trees had given way to blizzards of blooms, and the shadblow trees had burst out in clouds of white all over town. *And I've been all over town,* Thomas thought grimly.

He looked down at his legs to be sure they weren't wearing down to the bone. Old Francis was one person he never said no to.

As he passed through a fruit orchard that made a shortcut to the miller's yard, Thomas idly reached down to pluck a flax blossom of periwinkle blue whose seed had probably blown over from a nearby flax field.

It would be spring-luscious on the plantation right now, too. It was lambing time, and Patrick would be letting him help bring a few wet, frizzy bundles into the world. The hens would be having their broods of chicks, and if he were there, he and Patrick and the others would be running after them and bringing them back to the hen yard when they slipped away from their mothers.

I'm too busy for all that now, Thomas thought sadly. *And even if I did have time, there would be no one to do it with.*

A damp loneliness came over him, as heavy as the dew that sprinkled his boot tops as he crossed the grass to the cooper's stand. Just then, a small figure burst from the miller's house and raced across the road with a stick in her hand, rolling a large hoop in front of her.

It was that girl again. Thomas hadn't seen her since the day of the mud war. He didn't even feel like stomping over to her now and taking her stick or breaking her hoop, just to show her she should be careful who she laughs at through her window.

I'd rather play with her, he thought. *Or even her brother. I wonder where he is—*

But Thomas sighed and said, "Cooper! Is my barrel ready?"

There was another sullen session with Alexander that morning. Alexander was still reading *The Aeneid* aloud to him as happily as if they were taking a picnic, and Thomas was still fighting not to look too interested. It was all he could do not to complain when Alexander closed the book and brought out a square wooden box.

"Do you know what this is?" Alexander asked.

Thomas shook his head and sighed loudly.

"This is a puzzle of royal portraits."

He slid the top open and produced a stack of thin, white cards with oddly shaped edges. Alexander said, "As you can see, each of these pieces has the portrait of an English king or queen on it. The point of the game is to fit them together so that their edges match. Of course, if you know the order in which these monarchs reigned, it is much easier to put the puzzle together."

Thomas pushed it away from him. "My father wouldn't want me to know about English kings. He is a Patriot."

Alexander rubbed his chin thoughtfully. "You may be right. I shall have to discuss that with him. All right, then, in the meantime, let us study some science, shall we?"

He dipped his hand into his satchel and brought out a jar full of some liquid. He popped off the lid, pulled a tiny wand out of his vest, and, dipping it into the jar, began to blow bubbles with it.

"That isn't science!" Thomas said, snorting. "That's soap bubbles."

"Why do they float up like that, Thomas? Do you know?"

Thomas slapped at one and then looked down at his dripping finger.

"And why does it turn to water when you pop it? Answer me that one!"

"Who cares?"

"The enlightened people do, my boy. Be careful, because in this age to come, every man will have to do all he can to keep up. The learned will never be outwitted by those who still believe in old wives' tales. You don't want those other fellows to get the better of you, now, do you?"

Something about that lit a spark inside Thomas. "No!"

"Very well, then! Let me explain about these bubbles."

Later that afternoon, Francis was downstairs in the cellar, and Thomas was up in the shop alone. To his immense relief,

Francis had never asked him to go down the creepy staircase into the dark basement since that first day. He still kept an eye on the skeleton, but so far, no more had been added to the collection. Still, Thomas didn't do anything to get old Francis's head to turning red if he could help it.

I'd better get that rattlesnake root wrapped up for Mr. Wormeley's gout, he thought.

He was just putting the last of it into a box when the shop door opened. Without looking up, Thomas said, "Can I help you?"

"Maybe. And I think I can help you, too."

Thomas's head came up with a jolt. Henry Gates was strolling toward him, long arms flopping lazily at his sides. Thomas put the box aside and stiffened. There could be no fighting. His father had made that clear, and if old Francis caught him bloodying this boy's nose behind the counter, he'd be tossed down the cellar steps for sure.

"Don't worry," Henry said, propping his elbows on the counter. "I haven't come to pick a fight with you."

Thomas looked nervously over his shoulder toward the hall. "So what do you want?"

"I think you and I would make good partners," he said.

"Partners? In what?"

"In whatever we want. No one has ever been able to take me down the way you did the other day. With your strength and my wits, there isn't anything we couldn't manage together." The wide face cracked into its slit of a smile. "I say we let bygones be bygones and have a go at it."

He stuck out his hand for Thomas to shake, but Thomas regarded it doubtfully.

"What would we do?" he said.

"Oh, the usual things. Play ball with the boys at the carpenter's yard. They get pretty rough, but with you there, we could take them easy." Henry was looking very comfortable by this time, and Thomas felt himself leaning toward him across the counter and listening. Henry didn't seem so mean now. He almost looked like he could be . . . a friend. It had been so long since he'd had one.

Again, Thomas looked behind him and then lowered his voice. Henry pulled forward, the gleam of expectation in his hard eyes.

"All right," Thomas said, "but there is only one thing. My father. He told me not to—"

"Keep company with the likes of me, right?" Henry said. He shrugged. "If you want to let him push you around like that, I can't stop you. But I'm telling you, we can keep this a secret. It's more fun that way, anyway."

"Have you done that before?"

"Many times, and always with success." Henry wiggled his eyebrows. "When can you leave here?"

Thomas looked at the shadows that were slowly inching their way across the floor. Old Francis always closed the shop before dark so he wouldn't have to burn his candles. It was nearly that now. And then Thomas remembered the rattlesnake root he was wrapping.

"As soon as I get this ready I can leave to make a delivery," he said. "If you want to wait until then—"

Henry shrugged his bony shoulders again. "I'll just have a look around."

Thomas hurriedly cut the brown paper for the package. This very afternoon, he was going to have a friend to play with. It was as if someone had given him a present.

But Papa said I wasn't to get mixed up with such as Henry, he thought.

Thomas shook that off. Papa didn't know that Henry was really a friendly sort. You just had to get to know him.

With the thrill of coming adventure climbing up his backbone, Thomas cut off a piece of twine. Out of the corner of his eye, he could see Henry roaming around the shop.

"What's this?" he said, picking up a square jar with a piece of cloth secured tightly across its top. "Do you know?"

Thomas stopped tying and felt his chest puffing out. "Of course I know. That's rattlesnake root. We use it to treat gout and dropsy and sometimes fevers. Also, dog and snake bites."

Henry let out a whistle. "You surely know a lot. What's this thing?"

Henry swung a large leather object over his head.

"That's a sling for a broken arm," Thomas said. He glanced over his shoulder. "I'd put it down, though. Old Francis says never touch anything unless you're told to."

Henry gave a scoffing laugh. "Pretend you told me to. What's that old man going to do, anyway? You could take him down same as you did me."

Thomas tried to imagine himself wrestling Francis Pickering to the ground and laughed.

"You're getting the hang of it now," Henry said.

Thomas tied the last knot on the package. "Let's go now," he said. "As soon as I get this delivered, I'll be free."

But Henry didn't move toward the door. He scanned the room once more and said, "Does the old man use gold? They say it has healing powers, and I just wondered—"

"Yes!" Thomas said.

"I never believed that," Henry said. "I mean, who would

risk keeping a precious metal right in his shop except a silversmith? And I hear anyone who does can't even sleep nights, they're so worried about thieves."

"It's true," Thomas said. "He keeps it in that locked cabinet, back there."

Henry followed Thomas's pointing finger behind the counter.

"Don't go back there!" Thomas said. "No one else is allowed—"

"I just want to see it," Henry said. "Being of the lower class, I have never actually seen gold."

"I would show it to you," Thomas said. "Truly, I would. But Francis keeps the key on a chain 'round his waist."

Henry nodded wisely. "I would, too, if I had that much gold. How many jars?"

"Just one there," Thomas said. "The rest is in the cellar, on a shelf. I don't go down there much."

"Why not?"

"Come on," Thomas said nervously. "I have to make this delivery. Soon it will be dark, and we won't be able to play ball."

Henry sauntered to the door, still looking back at the locked cabinet. "I haven't time for ball tonight anyway."

Thomas looked quickly at the floor so Henry wouldn't see the disappointment flickering through his eyes. Henry cuffed him lightly on the shoulder. "But maybe tomorrow, eh?"

Thomas nodded and smiled. He finally had a friend, and suddenly Williamsburg didn't look so bad anymore.

‑ɪ‑ ✦ ‑ɪ‑

enry agreed to meet him at the carpenter's yard after his work the next day and promised that there would be a ballgame. Thomas's spirits were high as he raced home for supper. He even ducked his face in the water barrel behind the kitchen and brushed his hair before he appeared in the dining room. Mama glowed in the candlelight when he walked in.

"There is my handsome son!" she said in her bell-like way. "Isn't he becoming a fine young man, Mr. Hutchinson?"

"That he is," Papa said. "I've not been able to get more than a grunt out of Francis about his progress, but at least he hasn't tied him up in the cellar yet."

Thomas choked on his goblet of cider and had to plaster his napkin to his face.

"Well," Mama said, "then I think the surprise I have for you is very fitting."

Thomas put his napkin back in his lap and looked at her eagerly. *Surprise? Am I to be sent back to Hutchinson Homestead after all?*

Mama's gray eyes shone, and she put her dainty hand to the pearl choker at her neck in excitement. "Thomas," she said, "I have arranged for you to have dancing lessons."

Thomas's heart plummeted to the pit of his stomach. "*Dancing* lessons?"

"Yes! Even with the war going on, it is still important for you to learn the social graces. After all, you will own a plantation someday, and how will you win a wife to run your household if you cannot properly sweep her across the floor?"

Thomas looked helplessly at his father. *Wife? Household? Dancing lessons?*

But his father gave him no help. "That is wonderful news, my dear," he said to Mama. "When do these lessons begin?"

"Tomorrow. Right after your work at the apothecary. Thomas, you will have to come home and change into your finest clothes. You must learn to dance in them, of course. No one dances in leather breeches and homespun shirt!"

"I can't go tomorrow!" Thomas blurted out.

Mama's face froze as if he had just tossed his cider in her face, and Papa cleared his throat gruffly.

"And why not?" his father said.

Thomas opened his mouth to answer, and then he remembered his father's words. *"I don't think it wise for you to hang about with the likes of young Gates."*

Thomas firmly closed his mouth and shook his head.

"Then you will be ready come six o'clock, dressed in the red velvet," Mama said.

Thomas could only nod miserably. It was bad enough that he had to take dancing lessons at all. He could just imagine himself tripping over his own feet and ending up spread-eagle on the ballroom floor with a gaping hole in his red velvet breeches. But now he was going to miss Henry, too, and there was no way to get word to him. Even if he could get away on a delivery, he had no idea where the Gates's lived.

"Thomas, is there something wrong with the fricassee of chicken?" Mama said, her brows tucked together. "You've barely touched a bite."

Thomas looked blankly down at his porringer. He hadn't even noticed Esther's pathetic cooking tonight. Everything was suddenly tasteless.

"I heard the town crier again today," Papa said. "General Washington has sent the Maryland and Delaware regiments south to help South Carolina."

"Is that good?" Mama asked.

Papa shook his head ruefully. "Only if they can get supplies from the other states along the way. I hear tell the soldiers have gone as long as two days without food. That's the kind of thing I can't get Sam to listen to. I tell you, this is a foolish war."

Thomas didn't hear the rest. He had a battle of his own to fight.

He tossed and turned half the night, trying to think of a way to get out of going to dancing lessons. When he finally fell asleep, he dreamed that the girl with the melon-smile and the big white teeth stuck her foot out to trip him and then laughed while he turned into a skeleton on the floor of the Governor's Palace.

At least the real thing won't be as ghastly as my dream, he thought when he woke up.

He was so wrapped up in finding a plan that morning that he forgot to say no to Alexander and automatically answered the arithmetic questions Alexander fired at him while they were playing catch with three apples in the dining room. Thomas didn't realize until later that he had actually cooperated.

I'll make up for that tomorrow, he chided himself as he

hurried to the apothecary shop. *I have more important things on my mind today.*

Francis sent him on two deliveries, and each time Thomas stretched his neck to peer into gardens and pastures for some sign of Henry, but he was nowhere in sight. It wasn't until he was on his way back to the shop the second time that a memory flashed through his mind.

"Since when," Henry had said to him that first day, *"is an apothecary's apprentice better than a leathersmith's son?"*

Of course! Henry would be working at his father's shop, probably making bridles and travel bags this very moment. He could catch Henry there and tell him.

Thomas put on a burst of speed and ran the half mile to where he remembered the leatherworks to be.

He was wheezing like old Francis when he got there, but he didn't stop to catch his breath before he rushed in, setting the brooms hanging on the back of the door to swaying.

The man who looked up from the carriage armrest he was repairing was not Henry's father.

"Good day!" he said cheerfully, setting his red whiskers to life as he smiled. "What can I do for you today?"

"Tell me where Mr. Gates is!" Thomas exploded. "And his son!"

A shadow fell across the merry man's face. "I have no idea where either of the scoundrels are."

Thomas said, "Gates is the leathersmith, isn't he?"

The man chuckled wryly. "Not by a good deal! Oh, he told everyone at Chowning's that he'd owned a shop in Norfolk, but a traveler from those parts told us all later he'd worked in one for one day and been tossed out on his ear for stealing from the till."

"The till?"

"Where the money's kept, boy."

Thomas stood as if he were rooted to the floor.

"Is there anything else I can do for you?" Mr. Red Whiskers said kindly. "You surely look downhearted."

Thomas just shook his head and left the shop. Only the fear of Francis Pickering sent him running back to the apothecary's.

All afternoon the questions kept pounding in his head.

Why did Henry lie to me?

Is he someone I should stay away from, like Papa said?

If I see him again, what should I do?

There were still no answers by the time Francis closed the shop and Thomas walked unwillingly home. Even if there had been time, he didn't want to go to the carpenter's yard and tell Henry he knew he was a liar.

This time yesterday I thought I would be kicking a ball around this very minute, Thomas said to himself. *Now it will never happen.*

There was a great deal of fussing by Esther and squealing by Mama before Thomas was deemed fit for dancing lessons.

"I have been waiting for months to see you in this costume!" Mama cried.

Esther gave a disapproving tug at the silver brocade vest. "He's gotten into it not a moment too soon, far as I can tell," she said. "One more day and he'd have grown out of it for sure."

"That's my strapping, handsome son!"

"Mama, may I please go now?" Thomas said. He was in no hurry to get to the Raleigh Tavern, where the lessons were to be held, but anyplace was better than here with these two twittering over him.

Mama gave the stiff stand-up collar another pat and looked at him with mischief in her moist eyes. "Now don't you come home telling us you've had a marriage proposal from some darling little Virginia girl!"

Thomas gave a moan and took off down the stairs. There was still one possibility he hadn't thought of, and that was not going at all, hiding instead in someone's maze garden until it was over, and then . . .

But Papa was waiting at the bottom of the steps. When he saw Thomas, his square jaw softened into an unusual grin.

"Well, aren't you the dapper one!" he said.

Thomas looked down uncertainly at his red velvet breeches and ruffled cuffs. "Do I look silly?"

Papa patted him soundly on the shoulder. "Not for a moment!" he said, and then he glanced about and leaned close to Thomas's ear. "But you wouldn't be normal if you didn't *feel* a bit silly, what with all that primping and grooming they've done over you. Why don't I take you to the Raleigh in the carriage, eh? Avoid any taunts from the town boys." He chuckled softly. "I would hate to hear the tongue-lashing you would get from Esther if you were to get into a street brawl in *this* suit!"

For a moment, Thomas was grateful, and then his heart sank. This meant he'd have no chance to escape.

The Raleigh Tavern loomed like the jailhouse as Thomas climbed out of the carriage on the Duke of Gloucester Street and plodded in.

A very round woman in a gold satin gown rustled into the public dining room on a cloud of perfume. She asked his name, and he mumbled it.

"Come on, then, Thomas!" she said in a voice that would have put a mockingbird to shame. "We're ready to begin—here in the Apollo Room!"

She put her plump hand behind his shoulder to steer him toward the back of the tavern. "You didn't think we'd be holding the lesson in the public dining room, did you?"

"I didn't think about it at all," Thomas muttered irritably.

But the Gold Lady was already rustling to the front of the Apollo, where she turned, beaming, and faced a room full of children, all of them dressed in a rainbow of satins and taffetas. They were all paired up, boy-girl.

There's hope! Thomas thought. *They have no partner for me!*

As if she had read his mind, the Gold Lady waved a lacy sleeve and said, "There now, Caroline, you have a partner at last! This is Thomas Hutchinson."

As a girl in a yellow silk print dress got up from her chair at the side of the room, Thomas stared at her in horror.

It was that girl again—the one who had laughed at him at the well . . . the one who had snickered at him from a second-story window as he went by.

And he was going to have to dance with her.

She came to stand beside him without batting an eyelash, and when she stopped, her head came just to his shoulder. It was obvious that she had recognized him right away, for her chocolate-brown eyes twinkled at him as if she knew some joke about him that was going to make him the laughing stock of the room any minute. Thomas tried to copy his father's Look as he glared down at her.

"Now, then, children," the Gold Lady said. "You are about to embark on a great Virginia tradition, and it is only fitting that we should begin in this room. It is here that the great Thomas Jefferson himself danced with the fair Belinda—"

"I thought his wife's name was Martha," Caroline whispered.

Thomas looked down at her in surprise. She was standing very primly with her hands folded properly at her waist, but her fingers were twitching impatiently, as if she must do something with them within the minute or she would explode.

"—students from the College of William and Mary founded Phi Beta Kappa here in 1776—" the Gold Woman droned on.

Caroline rolled her brown eyes all the way up to her hair ribbon.

Thomas blinked at her. She hated being here as much as he did.

"The tavern is now owned by Mr. Wetherburn—"

"Only because he married the first owner's widow," Caroline hissed from behind her white kid glove. "He's done that twice, you know? Twice married the widows of tavern owners!"

Thomas could only stare at her stupidly. She stood first on one foot, then the other, and turned her head almost completely around to the back so she could make faces that mocked the Gold Lady's wide-eyed expressions.

"She ought to be careful," Caroline whispered to him. "Or those eyes are going to come popping right out of her head!"

Thomas had to choke back a laugh. He bugged his eyes out in imitation of the dancing teacher, and Caroline grinned at him until her 20 dimples deepened in each cheek.

"Now then!" the lady sang out, clapping her plump hands daintily. "Let us get on with the lesson."

"I had rather be playing ball," Thomas murmured.

"And I would rather being playing wa—"

Suddenly, Caroline clamped her teeth together and riveted her attention to the Gold Lady.

"Playing what?" Thomas whispered.

But Caroline shook her head and turned to Thomas to go into the deep curtsy the Gold Lady had just assigned. As she stood with her back straight, putting one foot slightly in front of the other, and bowing and tilting her head to the side a bit, something occurred to Thomas.

"What are you doing taking dancing lessons?" he said into her ear. "You're a servant."

She didn't look up as she said, "I could ask you the same thing."

"I told you, I'm not a servant."

"Neither am I."

"Then what were you doing at the well?"

"Probably the same thing you were doing," she said pertly as she rose. "Only I managed to actually get water into my barrel."

Thomas scowled. He could feel the back of his neck beginning to prickle. There was nothing to do but get her back for that.

"I hear this dance mistress is quite strict," he said. "She's been known to hit girls who make a mistake."

He watched her face as they stood side by side, and she put her hand on top of his. But she didn't flinch. In fact, he thought her brown eyes sparkled more than ever.

"Point your toe!" the Gold Lady warbled. "And we begin! My own sons will accompany you."

A round, bespectacled young man at the spinet and an identical one holding a tiny violin started to play, and the dance mistress clapped in brisk little strokes as she gurgled instructions that could still be heard over their thin tones.

"Step on one, sink down on two, step three, four, five. Sink down on six. Now backward!"

Backward! Thomas's head screamed. *I can barely do this forward!*

"Thomas Hutchinson!" Caroline hissed at him.

"What?"

"You're squeezing my hand like an onion! Are you trying to wrench the juice out of it?"

Thomas felt his face glowing red as he loosened his vice grip.

"Now forward once again!" the woman called.

Thomas lurched around and caught his toe on the heel of Caroline's dancing slipper. He grabbed at her sleeve to keep from going down, and to his horror he heard the ripping of silk.

Floundering, Thomas let go of her altogether and looked around frantically to see what everyone else was doing.

"Sink down on two—"

Thomas sank, but a beat too late. The rest of the dancers were already coming up. He jerked to catch up and brought his boot down squarely on Caroline's toe.

She stifled a squeal and looked up at him, her eyes flickering like candle flames.

"You're a clumsy thing, aren't you?" she said with a soft giggle lurking in her voice. "I'd as soon be dancing with one of our oxen!" Then she smiled like the sun and danced on. "Follow me," she whispered, "and we shall be out of here in no time."

But Thomas wanted to do anything but follow this snip of a girl who had laughed at him *again*, and this time without even trying to hide it. Every hair on his head felt as if it were standing straight up in anger.

He twitched his head from side to side, trying to get a better view of the other dancers. If her brother wasn't here watching her, he might try tripping her again.

"Where is your brother? Is he to learn to dance, too?"

Caroline cocked her head. "My brother learned to dance long ago. He's nearly 19!"

"No, not that brother. The other one. The brother I saw playing war games on North England Street."

Caroline let her white linen petticoat drop from her fingers and put them over her mouth. "'Oh," she said. "*That* brother!"

"Well, is he here?"

Her eyes twinkled as she took up her petticoat again. "You could say so."

Thomas gnawed at the inside of his mouth. There was nothing to do but endure this wretched girl. *I should have known better than to think I actually liked her*, he scolded himself.

The dance lesson went on so long that Thomas was certain it was midnight by the time he dashed through the public dining room and out onto the Duke of Gloucester. It was surely dark enough to be midnight, but Thomas wasn't bothered by the night and its shadows. He just wanted to get home to his bedroom, where he could punch his pillow.

A voice hissed to him from a set of stone steps that curved down from the street.

"You!" it said. "Apothecary boy!"

Thomas stopped and stared into the flame that shivered at the top of the stick of wood he carried.

It was Henry Gates.

✝ ✦ ✝

Chapter Twelve

"Where have you been?" Henry said. "I've been waiting since dark."

Something about the way the light from the firebrand played across his face made Thomas shiver.

"I'm sorry," Thomas stammered. "I had to . . . I had something else to do. My father made me."

Henry blew air noisily through his lips. "I can see I have a lot to teach you. Since you've finally showed up, let's go."

"Where?" Thomas said. His heart was starting to pound.

"How about the apothecary's shop? You have a key, don't you?"

"I? No!"

"The old man doesn't trust you enough yet, eh?" Henry nodded as if he knew some trade secret. "I can give you a few tricks, and before you know it he'll be giving you the key to the gold cabinet!"

"Why would I—?"

But Henry took him roughly by the arm and talked over his words as he half dragged him down Duke of Gloucester.

"Another night, then," Henry said. "I'll walk part of the way home with you. And don't worry, I won't let your father see me. I'm very good in shadows."

All right, Thomas thought, heart still thundering in his chest, *he'll walk part way, I'll say good-night, and then I'll think of some way to stay away from him—*

"You haven't answered my question. Where have you been all evening?"

"Dancing lessons," Thomas muttered.

An ugly laugh burst from Henry.

"It isn't funny!" Thomas said.

"Are you going to jump me again?"

Thomas shrugged.

"What's the matter, partner?" Henry said. He nudged Thomas hard on the shoulder.

"I'm just tired of people laughing at me. And when it's a girl—"

"Wait!" Henry curled his fingers around Thomas's arm and yanked him to a stop. His eyes bored in. "You say a *girl* laughed at you?"

"Well, yes."

"Who was she?"

"I don't know. Caroline somebody. She lives in the miller's house."

"Caroline Taylor. Ah, well, my father has had it in for the Taylors for a long time. There is no such thing as an honest miller, you know. And this family is more evil than most, because they're—"

"I don't think she's evil exactly," Thomas said quickly.

"She laughed at you, didn't she? But I warrant you, she'll never do it again—not after you and I get through with her."

Thomas felt his mouth go dry. A few minutes ago, he could think of nothing else but how to get even with the girl with the melon smile. But he didn't think what he had in mind was anything like what was brewing behind Henry's hard, stony eyes.

"That's all right," Thomas said. "You don't need to do anything to help me."

"Oh, but I do. We're partners, remember? Besides, you'll make it up to me." Henry wiggled his eyebrows and pulled Thomas on down the street. "Tomorrow is Market Day. The Taylors always do their own marketing. Meet me behind Chowning's Tavern after dinner. We'll find Mistress Taylor."

Thomas licked his dry lips. "And do what?"

"Leave it to me. I'll have a plan by tomorrow." Henry slapped him playfully on the back. "I'd better slip back into the shadows now before the high and mighty John Hutchinson catches you with me, eh? G'night, now."

On Market Day, people from all over brought their wagons to Williamsburg, and the shouting and the selling began in Market Square, across from the courthouse on the Duke of Gloucester Street. Booths and carts were set up for selling everything from onions to brooms, from tobacco to livestock, from land to slaves.

But Thomas paid little attention to the makeshift cloth roofs that went up on skinned branches to form shelter for the day for farmers selling their goods. He barely noticed the servants with big baskets over their arms or the black slaves with even bigger ones balanced on their heads, arguing with the farmers because their apples were bruised or their eggs weren't fresh.

Dodging the wagons with their farmer drivers waving their hats at each other, he got to the corner of Boutetourt Street, looking catty-corner at Market Square and waited for

Caroline so he could yell, "Run! Run away—before Henry Gates gets you!"

He felt as if he were in a cage and couldn't find the door. Caroline had annoyed him and embarrassed him, but he didn't really want to hurt her. Yet how was he to tell Henry Gates that? Last night he had seemed so much meaner than before.

As Thomas continued to search the Square, his eyes snagged on a familiar figure with broad shoulders standing in front of a cart that was hung on all sides with military uniforms.

Thomas took two steps backward and slipped behind a tree. Any other time, Thomas thought, he'd have jumped at the chance to see Sam. Normally, he'd have knocked down every housewife in Williamsburg to get to him.

But not today, he moaned to himself. *What if he sees me playing some trick on Caroline? Worse, what if he spots me hanging around with Henry Gates? He's sure to tell Papa.*

"*Psst!*" a harsh voice hissed. "I thought I told you *behind* the tavern."

Thomas turned around to see Henry leaning on the split-rail fence, looking tall and menacing.

"Oh," Thomas said lamely.

Henry took his arm. "No matter. The plan is so simple that I can tell it to you right here."

Thomas looked back to the uniform cart and sucked in some breath. For the moment, Sam had his back turned. It was time to try the only way he had been able to think of to get out of this.

"I don't think I should be seen with you, Henry," he said. "What if my father is about?"

"Your father—the great and wealthy John Hutchinson—comes to Market Day?" His mouth slashed open into a jeer.

"He's all over town," Thomas said. "He's responsible for Williamsburg."

"If he's so responsible, why does he let certain evil scoundrels continue to live here?" Henry shook that off quickly and said, "But not to worry. This will be over before your father can peek his head out of the courthouse. Look, there is our victim now."

A chill went straight up Thomas's spine.

Victim?

Thomas's thoughts tripped over each other like his own nervous feet. There, standing before a cart at the corner of Market Square, was Caroline Taylor. She was fingering some colored ribbons that hung from the cart, her mob cap snowy white over her sandy hair, a wide basket slung in carefree fashion over her arm.

"She's done with her shopping," Henry said, his hot breath close to Thomas's ear. "See the cover over her basket? All her goods are in there—and soon they shall be ours."

"What?" Thomas asked.

"Shhh! *You* go up behind her and pull her cap down over her eyes, and *I'll* grab the basket and run."

"But—"

"You go on to the apothecary shop. You can practically be there before she gets her wits about her to get her cap off. I'll meet up with you later."

"I don't think we should—"

"Of course we won't do it right there in the Square," Henry said. "She should be crossing the street to go home—right *now!*"

Henry's eyes glittered like a cat's as Caroline made her way toward them, swinging her basket contentedly beside her and skipping a little as she looked up to enjoy the redbud trees now in full pink bloom.

Thomas squeezed his eyes shut tight. *Please, please, don't let Sam see me.*

But just then Henry gave him a shove, and Thomas stumbled out into Caroline's path. Her brown eyes met his blue ones and sparked to life.

"Hello, Tom," she said brightly.

"Hello," Thomas said—like a piece of wood.

"Do it!" Henry hissed from behind him. "The cap, stupid oaf!"

Caroline dimpled. "I think he's talking to you."

Thomas darted his eyes once more toward the Square. Sam was gone!

With a jerk, Thomas reached up and snatched Caroline's mob cap down over her eyes. She sent up a squeal and reached her empty hand up to pull it back. Henry swooped in and grabbed the basket from the other hand.

But as Thomas watched in amazement, the cloth cover on the basket arose as if it were alive, and something very large and furry burst from under it, screeching louder than Caroline herself was doing.

"What—?" Henry hollered.

Before he could get out the rest of his sentence, the contents of Caroline's basket landed on his shirt front with 10 claws that ripped it down in strips and came back up for more.

"Get off me, wretched cat!" Henry screamed, dropping the basket with a thud.

But the fat orange cat had other plans. She smacked Henry's face and left him with four red, oozing stripes before she gave one last hiss and tore off behind Chowning's Tavern.

"Save your cat, Caroline!" Thomas cried as Henry tore after the animal. "Henry Gates will have her down the well for sure!"

"Don't worry, Tom," she said. "Martha will be asleep in the middle of my bed before that nasty Gates boy gets his breath."

Thomas stood with his mouth hanging open.

"Is the matter settled now?" Caroline said, shaking out her cap and tucking her hair back under it.

"What do you mean?" Thomas said.

"You only did that to teach me a lesson about laughing at you, didn't you?"

"It wasn't my idea!"

"You hated it when I laughed at you, admit it."

Thomas narrowed his eyes at her. "If you knew I didn't like it, why did you do it?"

"Because," she said, sniffing, "I think it's silly for a big, strong boy like you to be so uppity that he can't even laugh at himself." Caroline opened her brown eyes wide. "If I couldn't look in a glass and laugh at this face of mine, I would be in a good deal of trouble, Tom Hutchinson!"

"You don't have a funny face!" Thomas said.

She brought it close to his so fast that he had to step back. "Then you haven't had a proper look at it. Go ahead, get a good chuckle out of it. I don't mind."

Thomas crossed his arms. "You can honestly say you don't care if people laugh at you?"

"What good is it going to do me to get angry? That only makes them laugh harder."

"They don't laugh when I threaten to punch them."

"Oh, that's right. I've seen you double up your fists before."

"No, you haven't. I wasn't going to bother with you at the well that day."

"I wasn't talking about that day . . . but no matter. Do you want to be friends now or not?"

Thomas looked at her suspiciously. "Why would you want to be friends with me? I thought you said I was a bully."

She shrugged happily. "You only fancy yourself to be a bully. You're nothing like Henry Gates and you know it."

At the mention of the name, Thomas's mouth went dry again. "I thought I was, but he does really bad things . . . evil things."

"I know. He and his father have hated my family ever since they came to Williamsburg. My father says he doesn't think there's anything they wouldn't do to us if they had the chance. They're cowards, though. Have you noticed?"

"No, but I've noticed I'm a coward," Thomas blurted out.

"Oh, you are no such thing! Don't be a silly."

"I was afraid to tell him I didn't want to be his partner anymore."

"So be my partner instead. I can be just as much fun as any boy."

Thomas looked at her. She was probably right. He hadn't wanted to hit someone or kick anything since he'd been talking to her. But still—

"Meet me at the miller's yard tomorrow, right about this time," Caroline said. "I'll prove it to you. If I can't, we'll go on just as before, as if we didn't know each other."

Thomas thought about it. It might be better than being alone.

"I'll be there," he said.

Thomas had been so tangled up in worrying about dancing lessons and avoiding Henry Gates that he'd neglected his campaign to get rid of Master Alexander. When he came downstairs to the dining room for his lessons the next morning, he decided he'd better get back to it. The teacher was getting much too comfortable here.

"What silly game do you have for me to play today?" Thomas said in his best sulky voice.

But Alexander just took *The Aeneid* out of his satchel and slid it across the table toward Thomas.

"I'm sorry, Thomas," he said in a dead voice. "I haven't the stomach for games today. You'll have to do your own reading."

Thomas watched as Alexander turned and went to stand in front of the window. He studied the straight, slim back for a minute before he said, "What's the matter?"

Alexander glanced over his shoulder at him, his eyes lit with surprise. "What did you say?"

"Nothing."

"Oh," Alexander said tightly. "For a moment I thought you'd asked me what was the matter."

Thomas shrugged. "I suppose I did."

"Truly? You truly spent a moment thinking about someone besides yourself?"

Thomas looked at him sharply. There was no shine in Alexander's brown eyes, no dimple in either cheek. He wasn't teasing. Thomas waited for the anger to prickle up the back of his neck, but it didn't come.

"Do you really want to know what the matter is?" Alexander asked.

"Well . . . " Thomas stammered. "It just seemed odd. I've come to expect when I walk in the door that you'll toss some piece of fruit at me or have me searching the house for things that are parallel or some other such thing." He took a big breath. "Today, you . . . "

"What? I'm so wrapped up in my own concerns that I don't have time to do what is expected of me?" Alexander said. He laughed, but there was no humor in it. "That is how I feel every day, Thomas Hutchinson. I come in here eager to share the excitement of learning with you, but you are so entwined in yourself that you can't learn. You can't even laugh. Not even at yourself."

Thomas looked at him sharply. That sounded strangely like something else he'd heard lately.

"A war is being fought," Alexander said almost bitterly. "Its aim is that children like you will be allowed to grow up thinking and acting and living their lives as free men. But children like you are angry and frightened and spoiled and godless. The idea of your being free quite frankly scares me to death!"

"It scares me, too!" someone cried out in anguish.

The words hung in the air for several seconds before Thomas realized who had said them.

It had been Thomas Hutchinson himself.

✠ ⛦ ✠

lexander's face softened. "Why, Thomas? Why are you afraid?"

Thomas tried to shrug and turn away, but Alexander took him by both shoulders and turned him to face him squarely. "Tell me, please!"

"I'm scared because I can't do it!" Thomas said with misery in his throat. "I can't do any of it!"

"Any of what?"

"I can't be smart and holy like Clayton! I can't be powerful like Sam! Francis Pickering wishes I were older and quicker and not so clumsy. I'm a disappointment to Papa. I can't stand up to Henry Gates. I even found a *girl* who can outwit me. How am I supposed to run a plantation—or a country? I can't, I tell you!"

Thomas couldn't hold back the tears. Alexander nodded, as if Thomas had pulled the very words from his mouth. He handed him a handkerchief from inside his vest and turned toward the window while Thomas loudly blew his nose.

When Alexander turned around, his dimples were back.

"I think there may be hope for this new nation yet," he said.

"Why?"

"Because its young may be brave enough to say what every

105

man in the 13 colonies is probably thinking this very minute. We're all scared, and not a one of us is sure he can do it."

"Are you?" Thomas asked. And then he pulled back, for Alexander sprang across the table and grabbed his hand and pumped it excitedly up and down.

"There is indeed hope!" he cried.

Thomas looked at him blankly.

"Do you realize that that is the first time you have asked me a question in all the weeks I have been trying to teach you? I told your father if we could get you started asking questions, we might be able to shake you out of your stubborn silence and get you to learning. He reported that you've asked him exactly one—what does *curmudgeon* mean. I came in here this morning ready to give up. You hadn't shown a spark of interest with me that I didn't trick you into, and I was going to go to your father and resign this very day."

He did some kind of jig in the center of the room and then started to rummage in his satchel.

"But I'm here to stay now, young Thomas, because just this instant you turned into a student."

Thomas nearly hurled himself on the floor to kick and scream. *I was so close, and now I've lost! Instead of running him out, I've made him stay!*

"Oh, and by the way—" Alexander looked up from the satchel, honey-colored hair nearly standing on end "—to answer your question, no, I'm not sure I can handle independence and the building of a new nation either. I'm frightened out of my wits, but there is only one way to keep from being dragged under by that. Learn. Learn all you can. And your father is right, learn not just about the things I'm teaching you here, but about people, about the world . . . about God."

The urge to throw a tantrum right there in the dining room faded as if it had been blown away. In its place, a question crept into Thomas's mouth.

"But what if I can't—?"

"There is no *can't*," Alexander said. "There is only *try*. There is no failure when you've done your best. God will fill in the rest." He cocked an eyebrow at Thomas. "And I know you haven't even begun to show me your best, have you? You can probably read rings around most boys your age, and you're going to prove it to me." He slid *The Aeneid* across the table. "Go on."

Slowly, Thomas picked it up and flipped through the pages until he found the place where Alexander had left off. He frowned at the words, and Alexander laughed out loud.

"You're quite the actor, young Hutchinson," he said. "But I'm not easily fooled. Go on, read."

And so Thomas did, until the bell rang for dinner. When he looked up, Alexander smiled merrily.

"You're a sly one, Thomas," he said. "But the game is over. Let's get on with the game of learning now, eh?"

All through dinner, Thomas waited to get angry over the mess he'd made of things, but it never happened.

In fact, Esther's boiled ham didn't taste quite as dry as usual, Mama didn't fuss with his shirt collar, and Papa never once gave him The Look. When Papa asked "What did you learn today?" he answered at once, "There is no *can't*. There is only *try*. There is no failure when you've done your best."

His parents exchanged smiles across the table.

It had felt good to see them smiling their approval.

So Thomas's blood was flowing at a merry clip when he finished his afternoon chores and dashed off for the miller's yard. There was just time before he had to race off to work to meet Caroline and find out what "proof" she had that she could be as much fun as any boy.

North England Street was after-dinner sleepy as Thomas slowed to look for Caroline, but she was nowhere in sight.

Is this some kind of trick? he thought, scowling around the yard with his eyes. *If she thinks this is what boys do to have fun, she surely has a lot to learn about us.*

Just then there was movement in the direction of the miller's backyard, and Thomas almost called out, "Caroline! Over here! Hurry!" But it wasn't her. It was her brother again—the one Thomas had run into in the mud battle, the one with the smile and big white teeth identical to his sister's.

Why does he always go about in that mask and scarf? Thomas thought. *That's fine for a war game, but there's no one else to sling mud at today.*

Suddenly, Thomas scrambled up and made his way quickly to the puddle. If this Taylor boy thought he was going to catch Thomas Hutchinson unaware, he didn't know whom he was dealing with. Thomas scooped up two handfuls of mud and waited behind the wagon wheel.

He could see the Taylor boy's shoes moving toward him as if they were about to break into a dance. When they got to the edge of the yard, they stopped.

If he turns the other way, I can slip right past him, Thomas thought. *And if he sees me, no matter. I'm armed.*

The feet did turn in the other direction, and Thomas was about to drop his mud and scurry around the edge of the miller's yard when another thought came into his head.

What's to keep me from taking him by surprise?

Slowly, stealthily, Thomas rose from his crouch, hands still clutching his blobs of mud. With one mighty thrust of his arm, he pelted one of them right into the center of the Taylor boy's back. The boy whirled around, and Thomas caught him dead in the middle of the face.

A shriek went up, but not one of anger. There was sheer delight in the boy's voice as he dove for the nearest puddle and armed himself. Thomas dug for more mud and slung it almost before he could get it into balls suitable for pelting, but not before the boy got in two good shots at him.

Thomas's first reaction was to get angry and throw harder, but every time he hit the boy with another missile, the boy hooted with high-pitched laughter as if the mud were made of chocolate. Before he was hit too many more times, Thomas found himself laughing, too.

In Thomas's experience, throwing mud never stayed interesting for very long before you had to think of a new twist. The boy was way ahead of him. He hurled one especially well-aimed ball and then turned tail and ran.

Thomas smeared the mud out of his eyes and took off after him, shouting joyfully, "I'll get you! See if I don't!"

The boy was smaller and certainly quick, but Thomas's legs were stronger and could plow through the mud better. In five or six strides, he was able to grab the boy around the calves and tackle him. They rolled over, shrieking, in the mud. Thomas, of course, was able to pin the boy in two easy grabs.

"Are you having fun?" the boy said, smiling the big-toothed Taylor smile.

"Yes!" Thomas cried. "And I'm going to have more fun tearing off this mask!" Playing the victor for all he was worth, Thomas yanked off the mask, and with it came the scarf. A head full of long, silky, sandy-blond hair tumbled down into the mud, and round, brown eyes danced with glee.

Thomas had never felt himself move so fast as he scrambled off of her and got to his feet. He knew his eyes were bulging out farther than the Gold Lady's ever had.

"You!" he cried.

She came up on one elbow, still grinning. "I told you I could be as much fun as any boy," Caroline said.

"You tricked me! You made me believe you were your brother!"

"Oh, don't start getting uppity again," she said as she pulled herself up from the mud. "I didn't *make* you believe any such thing. You just looked at me and decided I was a boy. But appearances can be deceiving."

Thomas frowned. Where had he heard that before?

"You already admitted you were having fun, Tom," Caroline said. "You can't take it back now."

Thomas looked at her, with her hair straggling down like a horse's tail and the mud turning her face brown except in the exact spot where the mask had been. He couldn't help himself. He started to laugh.

"What's so funny?" she said, still grinning.

"You!"

"And were you thinking you looked like the Duke of Gloucester himself?"

"I'll warrant I look better than you do!" Thomas said.

"Then I shall have to see what I can do about that!" Caroline leaned over and slathered her hands with mud and then smeared it all over the front of his shirt.

"Wretch!" he cried happily.

"Scoundrel!" she answered, head thrown back in laughter.

Thomas got a palm full of his own mud, dumped it on her

hair, and took off running. But at the end of the block, he came to a stop so abruptly that he left ruts in his wake.

"What's the matter?" she asked.

"I'm supposed to be at work now! Old Francis will turn me into a skeleton if I come in dragging mud all over the apothecary shop!"

In a panic, he dug his fingers into the mud on his shirt to drag it off.

"Well, we can't have you being turned into a skeleton," she said. "Not now that we've just become partners. Come on, I can fix you up."

"But I shall be late!"

"Not if you hurry. Come along, then!"

Thomas followed Caroline toward her backyard at a gallop and watched her snatch up a leather bucket from a stack of them on the way. They stopped at a large water barrel just outside the laundry building, and Caroline sank the bucket into it.

"Close your eyes and hold your breath," she instructed.

Thomas did, and she poured the pail over his head—four times—until he was standing in a puddle and his clothes were sopping wet. But he was clean.

"Here," she said. She retied his hair and smoothed the top with her fingers. "It's a warm day. If you run and stay in the sun, you should be near to dry before you get there."

Thomas nodded gratefully and took off across the yard. When he stopped at the gate to look back, she was still watching.

"Meet me at dark, can you?" he said.

"Where?"

"At the corner!"

She nodded happily. Thomas found himself grinning as he ran down Nicholson Street.

Even if old Francis stripped him down to a skeleton today, he could die happy. After all, he'd finally found a partner.

Chapter Fourteen

The month of April flew by like the flocks of birds that had suddenly turned the world bright.

The mockingbirds sang all night, but that didn't bother Thomas. Neither did Henry Gates . . . because he didn't show his face around the apothecary shop after the day he made off with Caroline's basket.

In fact, nothing seemed to bother Thomas as much as it used to. Not even Alexander. The reading and writing and ciphering were soaring through Thomas.

He was even beginning to like old Francis Pickering. When Thomas thought about it, he realized that the turnabout there came in a very odd way.

He was sweeping up the glass from a bottle he'd broken when Mistress Wetherburn's slave girl, Cate, came into the apothecary shop and propped her elbows comfortably on the counter.

"Mistress Wetherburn say that cough still keepin' her awake at night," she said. "I personally never hear it, and I sleeps right in the next room case she have a notion that she need somethin'. But she say Francis Pickerin' ginger remedy the only thing keep her from dyin'."

"Dyin'," Francis scoffed. "The woman's sure to outlive us

all. Hutchinson! Get ready to wrap up Mistress Wetherburn's ginger cough remedy."

Glad to abandon the broom, Thomas brought some newspaper and twine over to the counter and watched.

He'll put in ginger, Thomas thought, *and a little licorice to sweeten the taste and coat her throat.* Just last week he'd started playing a guessing game with himself to see if he could name the things Francis would put in a medicine before the apothecary reached for the jar or pot. He had been right nine times out of the last 10 tries, so maybe he wouldn't count this one. It was too easy.

But to his surprise, Francis picked up the container marked *ginseng*, which was right next to the *ginger* in Francis's precise alphabetical arrangement.

Ginseng? Thomas thought as Francis began to measure it out. *We use that for people who are so tired they can't get out of bed.*

Thomas glanced uneasily at Cate. She was on the other side of the shop, admiring Francis's china apothecary jars.

"Ginseng, sir?" Thomas whispered to the old man.

"Ginseng!" he burst out. "What do I want with ginseng? If she takes that, she'll be dancing the minuet at midnight!"

Thomas gulped as Francis poured in the licorice. "I know, sir, you've taught me that," he said carefully—visions of the skeleton clattering through his brain. "That's why I wondered why you put it in there with the licorice, instead of ginger."

"I did nothing of the kind!"

"Yes, sir, you did." Thomas swallowed hard and picked up the jar at Francis's elbow. "See here?"

Francis snatched the jar from him and brought it up close

to his face and peered at it with a ferocious frown . . . which suddenly faded into an instant of fear.

"So it is," he mumbled. "I must have mistaken . . ."

"An easy mistake to make, sir," Thomas said quickly.

"Humph. I don't think Mistress Wetherburn would be so kind after she spent a night chasing her tail." Francis fumbled with the jar, his hands shaking. "Fetch me the ginger, boy. And dump out this miserable concoction."

Thomas did as he said. As Cate skipped off with Mistress Wetherburn's ginger cough remedy under her arm, old Francis sank onto a stool and wheezed.

"I'm not seein' so well as I once did," he said. "But I didn't know it was that bad."

The old shoulders hunched over like a hawk's, and Francis Pickering seemed to shrivel before Thomas's very eyes.

"Isn't that why you have *me*?" he blurted out.

"What nonsense are you talkin'?" Francis said. "Have you discovered some cure for old eyes?"

"No, but I can read labels. I know what almost all of them mean now."

Francis's birdlike eyes shifted from Thomas to the shelves and back again. Slowly, a bony finger came up and jabbed at a bottle.

"Ipecac," Thomas said promptly.

Francis pointed to another.

"Seneca rattlesnake root."

The finger poked again and again, and Thomas answered.

"Rhinoceros horn . . . cinnamon . . . coriander . . . lavender."

When Francis's bony finger came to rest on the counter,

the gray head nodded until Francis's spectacles slid to the end
of his nose.

"I never thought I would find myself sayin' this, boy, but I
think you can be a great help to me. All right, then, you will
check behind me whenever you are here. Make sure I don't
make any grave errors, you hear?"

Thomas nodded. Then he watched in amazement as a
small wrinkled smile sneaked onto Francis's face. "I must
admit," Francis said, "I should like to have heard Cate's story
of Mistress Wetherburn doing a jig in the middle of her bed,
wouldn't you?"

Thomas grinned. "I would, sir."

Ever since then, Thomas had become Francis Pickering's
eyes whenever he was in the shop. Thomas still kept the
picture of the skeleton set firmly in his mind, but the dread
he'd always felt as he trudged up the Duke of Gloucester
Street on the way to the apothecary shop was gone now.

And then there was Caroline. She had been right. She
surely *was* as much fun as any boy.

Every evening when Thomas left the shop, he dashed to
the corner of North England and Nicholson Streets, where she
would be waiting for him. One of them would have the
evening's game already in mind, lest they waste any time before
the church bell rang for evensong and they had to hurry home.

One day it was ring toss, another day, marbles. Alexander
taught him how to make kites—a lesson in physics, he said—
and Thomas and Caroline spent a windy Saturday flying them
in a field behind the college.

Then there was the time when Otis carved him two
whistles, and Thomas and Caroline took turns hiding and
tracking each other by whistle in Williamsburg's shadows.

And there was the evening they stole into the abandoned gardens behind the Governor's Palace and played until it was so dark they couldn't see each other. The maze made up of hedges was growing over with weeds, but so much the better for scaring the wits out of each other.

One evening they were playing hide-and-seek there and Caroline had hidden so well that Thomas finally called, "Olly-olly-in-come-free!"

He waited by a dried-up fountain for what seemed like an hour before he heard a quivery voice call out, "Thomas?"

"Where are you?" Thomas said.

"Here," she answered.

Thomas had a queasy feeling in his stomach as he followed her echo. He'd known Caroline only a short time, but he already knew it wasn't like her to sound frightened.

"Here!" she called to him again.

By now he was beyond the maze and out of sight of the empty palace. His steps slowed, and he thought he heard water.

"I'm here, Caroline," he whispered. "Come on out now. The game's over."

"Psst! Here!" she said.

She waved her hand at him, and Thomas stared. Just behind the tree he'd started to lean on was a canal. Caroline was climbing out from under a bridge that went across it.

"All right, you win," Thomas said. "I would never have found you here."

Caroline scurried over to him. "I wasn't hiding from you. I was hiding from that man."

"What man?"

"The one who went over the bridge."

"Did you get a look at his face?" Thomas asked. "It wasn't Henry Gates, was it?"

"No! He acted like he didn't want anyone to see him."

"Where did he go?"

"Across the bridge, away from the palace. He's gone now. I waited until I was sure before I called you." She shook her blond head and tried to laugh. "It seems silly now. He wasn't scary or anything. I just wanted this to be our private place, you know?"

Thomas nodded.

Caroline sighed happily and stood up. "It's all right now. And by the way, Tom, isn't that a wonderful bridge I've discovered?"

Thomas had to agree. Alexander had shown him pictures of China in a book, and this bridge looked for all the world as if it had come straight from the Orient on one of his great-grandfather Josiah's ships.

"I think that bridge is just waiting for us to play on it," Caroline said.

"Well, come on, then!"

From then on, the bridge served as everything from a ship on the high seas during a hurricane to a mountain they had to climb to escape the wrath of a Prussian madman in a pointy helmet.

"You know such wonderful things to make games out of," Caroline told him one soft April evening as they sat high up in a poplar tree, swinging their legs down at a passing ox cart.

"I learned them from my teacher," Thomas said. It was hard not to puff his chest out and swing his legs a little more powerfully. But when he did, he lost his balance and had to grab at the tree trunk to keep from falling end over end to the street below.

"You're such a clumsy oaf, Tom," Caroline said, big white teeth shining in the dim light.

Thomas just grinned back. She was the only person in the world besides his brother Sam who could say something like that to him and not be in danger of at least a scowl from him, if not a strong shove.

But Thomas had to pause. *I haven't punched anyone in a long time*, he thought. *I haven't even wanted to.*

Not even at dancing school. Caroline had carried him through all six of their dancing lessons, before the Gold Lady had decided her students could hold their own at any courtly affair and had packed up her two sons and gone off to Fredericksburg to teach the children there.

"Poor devils," Thomas said to Caroline. "Perhaps we should ride there ahead of her and warn them."

"We could take one of my father's steeds and dash through the night," she said.

But since that was out of the question, they settled for a gallop with stick horses across the Chinese Bridge and added an imaginary attack by an evil Chinese emperor and his men in pointy helmets.

Life, it seemed, couldn't be better for Thomas. And one Sunday it got even better—at least for a little while.

✝ ✦ ✝

Chapter Fifteen

C lay had arrived the night before and was sitting at the breakfast table with Thomas and Papa when Mama sent down word that she had awakened with a cold and a cough and would not be going to church with them. Esther bustled importantly out to the kitchen to fix her a warm posset of milk and spices, and Thomas said, "Mama needs some licorice troches."

Clayton stared at him. "How did you know that?"

"I learned it from Francis Pickering."

"You learned it?" Clay said. "Did you say you *learned* it?"

"Now, Clay," Papa said kindly. "Don't antagonize the boy."

Thomas stopped in mid-bite. "What does *antagonize* mean?"

"It means Clayton will make an enemy of you if he doesn't stop."

But Clayton was still staring. "Father, he asked a question!"

"So I heard," Papa said. He smiled secretively at Thomas. "Does that surprise you, Clayton?"

"Does it *surprise* me? I'm flabbergasted!"

Thomas grinned at his father. "What does *flabbergasted* mean?"

Papa's laughter pealed out like the church bells. "It means your brother will soon be picking up the teeth that have fallen from his mouth in utter amazement!"

Papa sipped happily at his coffee, and then suddenly rattled the cup to its saucer. "I have an idea. Since your mother will not likely be coming down for dinner this afternoon, why don't we men take our meal at Wetherburn's Tavern after church? Perhaps we can spring Sam free from Professor O'Hara's chains long enough to join us."

Thomas could only stare, his lower lip hanging.

"What is it, Thomas?" Papa said, eyes twinkling. "Have you heard something about the food at Wetherburn's that we should know about?"

"Me?" Thomas said. "You want *me* to go with you?"

"Only if you promise not to trip and fall into the venison stew," his father said.

Papa led Thomas, Sam, and Clayton to the large public dining room in Wetherburn's Tavern, where cherry wood dining tables and cut crystal gleamed in the sun that streamed through the blinds.

"The Great Room," Sam said to Thomas in a low voice. "It's the finest in town."

As they seated themselves around a large round table in the center, a few other men came in for the midday meal. Some of the men were planters Thomas vaguely remembered from when he was small, some of them church vestrymen he'd seen filing in and out of his father's study at home.

"'Tis quiet today," Papa said. "I remember when this room would be bustling with the likes of Thomas Jefferson, Richard Henry Lee, Patrick Henry—even George Washington himself."

"We're not good enough company for you, Father?" Sam asked.

Thomas looked up quickly. There was no sparkle in Sam's voice. His shoulders were stiff with tension, just like Papa's. "I could be as much a Patriot as any of them."

"And I'm sure you will be," Papa said, "as a statesman, not a soldier."

"But I shall never be elected to office if I don't join in the fight—"

"Thomas," Papa interrupted, "have you ever eaten off of Chinese porcelain?"

"No, sir," Thomas said, glancing nervously at Sam.

"Well, you shall have the pleasure today. Wetherburn serves on the finest you'll ever see."

Papa shot Sam The Look, and Sam sat back in his chair. The silent anger was as thick as the soup the slave set in front of them.

"Chicken and asparagus," Papa said.

Clayton nodded to Thomas. "Enjoy it. You'll be eating Esther's cooking again for supper."

Thomas didn't have to be told. In spite of the uneasy cloud that had settled over the table, his silver porringer was empty before anyone else's, and he eyed the rest of the dinner fare with drool forming at the corners of his mouth. Soon the table was groaning with chargers piled high with turkey, veal, chicken, lamb, and venison. Even Sam pulled forward in his side chair again and joined in the merriment. The cloud disappeared.

"Save space in your stomach for apple tarts and ginger cakes," Sam said as Thomas reached for his third slab of roast lamb.

Just then, Xavier Wormeley waddled over to their table and put his plump hand on Papa's shoulder.

"A fine looking family you have here," he said.

John Hutchinson stood up and motioned him to one of the empty chairs.

"Xavier! Please join us! You know my sons Clayton and Samuel, but I don't believe you've met my youngest, Thomas."

Thomas started to say "It's nice to see you again, sir," but Xavier Wormeley slid his reddened poke hole eyes over Thomas and nodded blankly.

"Pleasure to meet you," he said, without an ounce of pleasure in his voice.

Thomas felt as if he'd been stung. *He doesn't even know me*, he thought. *It's as if he came into the shop every week and saw no one at all behind the counter.*

There was a nudge at his elbow, and Thomas looked up at Sam. His brother nodded toward Mr. Wormeley, who was already firing questions at Papa as if he were before himself and the other 23 magistrates in the Gloucester County Courthouse.

"Listen carefully," Sam hissed to him.

What has this to do with me? Thomas thought.

"What have you done about this Loyalist situation, John?" Xavier Wormeley asked.

"What situation?" Papa said, calmly selecting an apple tart from the grand array of desserts in the middle of the table.

Xavier's jowls quivered. "You know exactly what I am speaking of. We still have people who remain loyal to King George living here in Williamsburg!"

"And do they not have the right to do so?"

"No more than they have the right to destroy the war effort and be the enemy of this new country!"

"Who has done that?" Clayton said.

"We don't know," Xavier bellowed. "They do it in secret!"

Papa laughed. "Xavier, it is we Patriots who are considered the traitors!"

Xavier shook his head. "We are a country of our own now, John. Anyone who is of a mind to do anything against it is a danger to us all. Yet you let them live here!"

"What do you suggest I do, Xavier?" Thomas's father said. His voice was still calm, but Thomas noticed that he hadn't taken a single nibble of his apple tart.

"Since the war started, every state has authorized exiling Loyalists and seizing their property!" Xavier said. "A suspected Loyalist can be summoned before the committee and asked to show cause why he should be considered a friend to the Americans. If he cannot give good reason, he should at the very least be fined 2,000 pounds. I would rather he be sentenced to two years in the appropriate jail—"

"Or flogged," Papa said. "You missed that one, Xavier."

Papa was shooting The Look all over the place, and Thomas wanted to lower himself under the table. *Why did he have to join us?* Thomas thought as he glared at Xavier Wormeley. *Everything was going so well.* For the first time in weeks, Thomas's neck began to stiffen with anger.

"It is your responsibility to help keep this town safe, John!" Xavier was nearly shouting now. "And I myself cannot feel safe when there are Loyalists still living among us."

"I know who they are," Papa said with strained patience in his voice. "I am aware of their activities. I have found nothing that is the least bit alarming or threatening. Some of them are vital to the survival of Williamsburg."

Xavier leaned in like a cat homing in on its prey. "What if one of your sons were involved? What if this one—" he pointed wildly at Thomas "—were fighting for this country in the Virginia Militia and one of your Loyalist friends told the British where his regiment was camped—and he was killed!"

"Enough!" Papa said finally. "I have no Loyalist 'friends.' I only allow them to live peacefully in this town, where they have built homes and raised families and carved out trades just as the rest of us have."

"Then you would not have a Loyalist as a friend?" Xavier said, still leaning.

"Of course not!" Everyone looked at Clayton, whose thin lips were trembling. "Forgive me, Father, for breaking in."

"It's quite all right," Papa said. "Go on."

"You would never ask such a question, Mr. Wormeley," Clayton said, "if you knew the kind of treatment my father and I have received at the hands of our Loyalist neighbors on the plantation. The things Carter Ludwell has accused us of—it boggles the mind."

"That is the point exactly," Wormeley cried, pounding his fist on the table so that Thomas's silverware bounced.

"No," said John Hutchinson. His voice brought everyone up in their seats, and silence fell on the group. "That is not the point. I have nothing to fear from Carter Ludwell nor any of the Loyalists who live in Williamsburg. I will not see a man hanged or flogged or exiled for what he believes. That is why I support independence but don't support the war. I will say it again, Xavier Wormeley. The Loyalists are not my friends, but I have no right to drive them from the city. Now, feast your eyes on these tarts and ginger cakes and let us go on to happier subjects, shall we?"

But Xavier Wormeley only sniffed and scraped his chair back from the table. Once he was back with his companions, jowls jiggling and sausage-shaped finger pointing, the

Hutchinsons' conversation turned to what Clayton thought the peach crop would be like this year. But most of the joy was gone for Thomas.

The rest of it disappeared as they all walked Sam back to the college.

Sam let his father and Clayton get ahead of them, and then he clasped Thomas's arm tightly.

"You heard what Papa said about the Loyalists," he said into Thomas's ear.

"Yes," Thomas said. He tried to pull his arm away, but Sam held fast.

"You understood the part about not being friends with them."

"Yes." Thomas stopped and looked Sam full in the face. "Why is it so important for me to get all this business about the Loyalists? Why were you nudging me at the table to listen to old Floppy Jowls?"

"Because you can't be friends with a Loyalist, Thomas."

Thomas snorted. "I don't intend to become friends with any of them! I don't even know any of them!"

"Oh, but you do."

Thomas shook his head. "I don't, Sam. What are you talking about?"

Sam brought his face close to Thomas's, his big shoulders towering above him. "I'm talking about that girl. That Taylor girl. She's a Loyalist, Thomas."

✝ ✝ ✝

Chapter Sixteen

Thomas felt as if he'd been struck by a snake.

"You look as if you didn't know that," Sam said.

"I didn't . . . because it isn't true!"

"Well, it's certain it is." Sam nudged him on down the sidewalk. "Her father is Robert Taylor, who owns the mill. The only reason no one has run him out of Williamsburg is because they need him to grind their wheat and corn into flour. Things are bad enough without having no bread."

Of course. Old Francis had mentioned "that Loyalist miller" the first day he'd worked in the shop, but he'd never tied them together. Thomas's heart started to pound.

"I don't care who her father is," he said stubbornly. "Caroline is no Loyalist."

Sam smacked Thomas lightly on the side of the head. "Don't be a fool, Thomas. She comes from a Loyalist family, and that's enough."

"I come from a Patriot family, and that hasn't stopped her from being *my* friend."

"Her father doesn't have anything to lose from it. Yours does."

Thomas's neck was so hot that he was sure it would catch fire any minute. "I don't care! I'll be friends with whoever I please."

127

Thomas's voice rose above the chattering of the birds, and Papa glanced over his shoulder from the steps of the Main Building of the college.

"You'd *better* care, little brother," Sam said tightly. "You heard Xavier Wormeley. The people in this town are suspicious enough of Papa for letting the Loyalists stay here. If you start running all over Williamsburg with the daughter of a known Loyalist, just think how that's going to look."

"We mostly play behind the Governor's Palace when it's almost dark," Thomas said. "No one will even find out we're friends."

Sam looked at him straight on, his blue eyes solemn. "I did."

"Samuel!" Papa called out. "Are you planning to talk Thomas's ear off?"

Sam plastered on a smile. "I'll be along in a minute, Papa!" he called out. He kept the smile on his face as he turned back to Thomas.

"I saw you with her on Market Day once. At first I thought you meant to try to run her out of town yourself, the way you pulled her cap down over her face. But then you hung about as if she'd cast some kind of spell on you. And I've seen you two those nights, prancing around on the bridge—"

"It was *you* watching us then!"

"Listen." Sam put both hands on Thomas's shoulders. "Don't get yourself—or Papa—into trouble. Think about someone besides yourself. We all have to. We have a country to run."

Thomas pulled his shoulders away and riveted his eyes to his boot tops. "I thought we were fighting so we could be free. Now you're telling me who I can and cannot have for friends."

The kindness snuffed out of Sam's eyes like candle flames. "I thought you'd changed, but it seems I was wrong. You're still as selfish as you ever were. God help you."

The heels of Sam's shiny black shoes rapped angrily across the stones as he strode away toward Papa and Clayton. Thomas felt as if a hammer were taking blows at his stomach.

I have *changed*, he wanted to shout after him. *I'll show you I have!*

And then he gnawed furiously at the inside of his mouth and clenched his fists at his sides.

All the next day, the thoughts nagged at Thomas. *What am I going to tell Caroline? Should I even meet her today? If Sam discovered us, who else has seen us running around together? What if Papa finds out? How can I keep that from happening?*

Only one thing was clear in his mind. Things were different now with Papa. Thomas was feeling as if he might in some small way be as good as Clayton or even Sam. Nothing—not even the only friendship he had—was going to get in the way of that.

"Hutchinson!" Francis wheezed from the doorway. "Would you stop that eternal daydreaming? There's someone coming up the step right now. I can't afford to lose a customer because your mind has left town!"

Thomas shook himself to attention and watched as a slight man about his father's age came cautiously in the door and closed it carefully behind him. The man was well-dressed and had his graying blond hair curled at the sides and tied back neatly in a cue at his neck. Most men who looked as well-to-do as he did sent servants to fetch medicines.

This man's wide mouth looked serious and concerned, and the eyes that met Francis Pickering's across the room were worried ones. Something, Thomas decided, was surely wrong at this man's house.

"What do *you* want?" Francis barked.

Thomas looked at him, startled.

"I know you have no time for me, Pickering," the man said. "And I wouldn't bother you if it wasn't an emergency. It's my wife—"

"You can buy patent medicines at the post office," Francis snapped again. He turned his hunched back to return to the examination room, but the man strode to the center of the room.

"I can't imagine you'd let an innocent woman die for politics, Mr. Pickering," he said.

There was a pause as old Francis peered at him over his glasses. Finally, he ran his hand over his thin, gray hair and sighed.

"Come in," he said in a tight voice. "Tell me what ails the woman." He sniffed and shuffled into the examination room. The man followed.

I wonder what that was all about, Thomas thought.

Seconds later, the man hurried back through the shop and out without a glance at Thomas. Within a few minutes, Francis himself came out and banged two containers down on the counter.

"Woman's gone and cut herself deep on a piece of broken glass," he said gruffly. "If they'd go on and leave town, they wouldn't have people throwing rocks through their windows. Lucky she wasn't killed."

"Someone threw a rock?"

"Here, take these. Tell them to put the salt petre in the wound to clean it out and then pack it with the salt of ammonia to keep it from rotting. You've seen me do it. Show them and then get back here, quick as you can. Take the back way, behind the bake shop. Don't let anyone see you."

"Where am I going?" Thomas said, his heart racing.

"To Robert Taylor's—the lousy Loyalist. Corner of Nicholson and North England."

All sense of adventure slid from Thomas's mind. He was going right to Caroline's house, right up the front steps and into her home. Surely she was going to expect him to sneak her a smile that said, *I'll meet you this afternoon. We'll play pirates on the bridge.*

Please, he said to that someone, *don't let her be there.*

In his hurry to get to Caroline in the past, Thomas had never paid much attention to the front of her house, which faced Nicholson Street. Now it loomed over him like a great cream-colored prison with 12 brown-rimmed eyes. It was much bigger than the Hutchinsons' Williamsburg house, and it seemed even larger than it was as he lifted the brass knocker on the heavy mahogany door. When the door opened, Thomas stepped back and gaped.

"Thomas, please come in!" said Alexander from the doorway. "We've been expecting you!"

He gripped Thomas's arm warmly and pulled him into the wide, white hallway.

Thomas barely heard the heavy door pound shut behind him. He could hear only the slamming of his heart against his chest.

"I knew you worked for the apothecary, of course," Alexander was saying, "but until I heard you were coming yourself, I had no idea you were Pickering's right hand. Please, come up stairs. She's in bed, poor woman. . . ."

The rest of Alexander's excited words were lost as Thomas followed him up the U-shaped staircase.

What is he doing here? Thomas thought. *Is he Caroline's tutor as well?*

He is a Patriot, isn't he?

Of course, Thomas scolded himself. His father wouldn't have a Loyalist in the house, teaching his son.

Alexander led him into a white-paneled bedroom, and Thomas squealed to a stop in the doorway. Caroline was standing next to the bed.

She didn't see him at first. She was busy wiping her mother's forehead with a cloth and pulling the dark-blue comforter up under her chin. Thomas considered whipping around and tearing off down the stairs, but Alexander pulled him into the room with an arm slung around his shoulder and said, "Mistress Betsy! Here's help for you!"

Caroline looked up and grinned the slice-of-melon smile. From the bed, a tiny pair of pale lips turned up from just above the comforter.

Thomas sighed and went toward her, careful to keep his eyes away from Caroline's. The frail-looking creature who peeped at him from the pillow had a face as delicate as a wren's, yet a thick halo of sunshine-colored hair spread out on the bed linen, enough for two heads.

Everyone seemed to close in behind him as Thomas held out the two containers and said, "I'm from the apothecary's."

"Pickering said there would be instructions," Mr. Taylor said.

"Oh." Thomas fumbled with the package of salt petre.

"You're to clean the wound with this and then pack it with—"
He held out the salt of ammonia.

"Oh, Robert," said the wispy woman in the bed. "You'll
never be able to do this! You'll faint right there on the floor,
sure enough."

Robert Taylor nodded ruefully. "You're right, my dear."

"Thomas, will you do it for us?" Alexander said.

Thomas looked at them all helplessly, with the picture of
being hung up by his thumbs in old Francis's basement stuck
firmly in his head.

"I'm not supposed to," he said slowly.

"Then she'll die!"

Everyone's eyes went to Caroline, who'd spat out the
words and then buried her face in the pillow next to her
mother's.

But I can't! Thomas wanted to say to her. *Old Francis will
have my skin! My father will be driven out of town! I'll be just
as much of a disgrace to the Hutchinsons as I ever was!*

Betsy Taylor ran an almost transparent hand across
Caroline's sandy hair. "There, there, sugarplum," she said.
"I've no intention of dying now."

Thomas had to swallow hard against a lump that suddenly
took shape in his throat. Mistress Taylor was just like his own
mama, soft and comforting even amid the fit Caroline was
throwing. What if Mama had been hurt by people just
because they didn't believe the way she did? And what if
nobody would help? And what if she died?

"All right, then," Thomas blurted out. "Show me the
wound, and I'll do it."

Caroline's head popped up from her mother's pillow with
the slice of a smile already spread across her face.

"Thank you, Tom!" she said, tears shimmering in her eyes.

But Thomas looked quickly away. *I'm going to be in enough trouble for doing this*, he wanted to tell her. *I just can't be your friend anymore.*

Betsy Taylor's nightdress sleeve was pulled back to reveal a gaping wound that made Thomas wince.

"We pulled out the glass," Alexander said quietly to Thomas as he stood by with a bowl of water. "It was a splinter as long as my little finger and twice as wide."

What were you doing here when it happened? Thomas thought.

But after that, he could only concentrate on cleaning the cut with salt petre and packing it with salt of ammonia. It wasn't hard, really. He'd assisted Francis in doing it at least 10 times.

Once the packing was in place and a piece of clean white linen was wrapped around Mistress Betsy's arm, Thomas cleared his throat and looked at Mr. Taylor. "You'll have to change that several times a day," he said. "And if it starts to turn black or smell . . . "

His voice trailed off. If that happened, the Taylors were lost. There wasn't a Loyalist doctor or apothecary in town to do whatever needed to be done.

"I have to go now," Thomas said quickly. "I'm late already."

There was a chorus of thank-yous, and Caroline's mother insisted on clinging to his hand as she smiled up into his face. He could feel Caroline trying to catch his eye, but he scurried out of the room without looking at her. If he could just get out of there, he thought, she would get the hint and it would be over without his ever having to tell her why.

Alexander saw him to the door and pumped Thomas's arm until he was sure it would come off in Alexander's hand.

"We can never thank you enough," he said, smiling broadly at Thomas.

"I don't understand why you—" Thomas started to say.

But out of the corner of his eye, he saw Caroline lingering at the stair rail above them.

"Never mind," Thomas said, slipping out the door.

He was almost to the shop when the footsteps behind him started to catch up.

"Tom! Tom Hutchinson, you stop right now!" Caroline called out behind him.

Thomas glanced over his shoulder. His toe struck a hole, and he sprawled to the ground with sand and pebbles immediately spraying his face.

"Serves you right!" Caroline said above him. "Acting as if I wasn't even in the room. Do you think you are such a proper doctor now that you have no need to notice me when you're about your important work?"

"No!" Thomas said. He got carefully to his feet and tested his bones to see if anything was broken.

"Stop pampering yourself and tell me what is going on!" Caroline said. She stomped her foot like an exclamation point.

The words exploded out of Thomas. "Why didn't you tell me your father was a Loyalist?"

Caroline stared. "I thought you knew."

Thomas felt his lip curling. "How would I know?"

"I thought *everyone* knew!"

"I only just moved here!"

The sentences were flying like angry balls being hurled back and forth.

"Why did you think I dressed up like a boy in a mask?" Caroline volleyed.

"To fool me!" Thomas threw back.

"You think pretty highly of yourself, Tom Hutchinson! I did it so someone—even those rough Patriot boys—would play with me. I'm the only Loyalist child left in town. Why else would I choose you to be my partner?" The brown eyes burned into Thomas, just like her words did. "I thought you liked me because I was . . . Caroline Taylor . . . as much fun as any boy!"

"I did!"

"Then what about now?"

The tossing of the angry balls came to a stop with a thud, and Thomas could only look down at his shoes.

"I can't be your friend," Thomas said, "because you're a Loyalist."

Caroline's face twisted, as if her lips didn't know which words to burst out with first. "You're a liar, Tom Hutchinson!" she spat out finally.

"I'm not! That's the reason! It would get my father into trouble!"

Caroline planted her hands on her hips. "Really? Then why doesn't it bother you to be my brother's student?"

Thomas stared at her stupidly. "What do you mean?"

"Alexander."

"What about him?"

"Alexander Taylor is my brother, you foolish boy!"

With that, she turned on her heel and marched off down Nicholson Street, leaving Thomas without a friend in the world.

✠ ⟡ ✠

Chapter Seventeen

As Thomas stood behind the shop, it suddenly seemed as if everyone he considered a friend was on the other side of a wall. Sam was disappointed in him now, and Francis would be when he found out Thomas had actually dressed Betsy Taylor's wound. And then there was Papa. Now he would have to tell him about Alexander.

Because surely he doesn't know, Thomas thought as he finally turned to stumble toward the apothecary shop. He wouldn't have a Loyalist teaching his son.

Of course Alexander would be dismissed at once—the very thing Thomas had worked so hard for at first. And the very thing that made the tears sting his eyes now.

Thomas squeezed his fists at his sides as he rounded the back of the apothecary shop and headed for the side door by the cellar stairs. *I have changed, Sam Hutchinson*, he cried inside.

But what good did changing do when it hurt more this way? It had been so much easier to let the anger race up the back of his neck until he punched some fellow's unsuspecting nose. Thinking about someone else . . . this was hard.

Thomas picked up a stone and was about to hurl it into the side of the shop when the side door swung open.

Francis is going out looking for me! Thomas thought wildly.

He dropped the stone and dove behind the hedge that bordered the shop. The door banged shut and a pair of clunky work boots thudded by Thomas's hiding place as if a stampede of horses were in hot pursuit. Thomas peeked cautiously through the leaves and watched the figure retreat into the stand of trees just beyond the shop. He felt his eyes start from their sockets.

The person—whoever he was—was wearing a black hood.

How odd, Thomas thought. *It's April. Too hot for a cape and hood. Only there was no cape. . . .*

"Hutchinson!" a voice blew out like bellows from inside the shop. "Where the devil are you?"

Thomas floundered out of the shrubbery and took the steps two at a time. Francis met him at the door.

"What was wrong with that man, sir?" Thomas said.

"What man?"

"The man with the hood," Thomas said. But by the way the red was running up old Francis's forehead, he wished he'd never started this conversation.

"There was no man with a hood in here," Francis said. "Only several dozen slave girls wanting things I had to waste my time fetching for them because you were out lollygagging around." He turned and tottered toward the examination room, still muttering. "The minute I think you've gotten some sense into that thick head of yours, you bungle it."

There will be no more bungling, Thomas thought fiercely. *I'll show them.*

But there was no smile of satisfaction to smother. Only sadness.

That evening at supper, Thomas was ready to split open with his news that Alexander Taylor was a Loyalist. His father had just sat down at the table with Thomas and his mother when Esther bustled in with a piece of rolled up parchment.

"Just delivered, sir," she said. "Someone from the Ludwell Plantation brought it."

John Hutchinson's eyes seared the paper, and his eyebrows came together over the bridge of his nose as if they were going to wrestle.

"Bad news, John?" Mama said.

"It could be . . . unless I nip it in the bud." Papa scraped his chair back from the table. "I'm sure your pigeon stew is delicious, Esther, but you must all excuse me. I have some business to attend to. I'm sorry there will be no Evening Prayer tonight."

Let me go with you! Thomas wanted to call after him. *I have something to tell you.*

But his father disappeared into the hall, and Thomas's chance to talk to him about Alexander vanished with him.

John Hutchinson was still out when Thomas went to bed that night. It was a soft, late April night, and Thomas opened his window before he fell into a fitful sleep. The sound of the front door closing brought him straight up in bed.

Thomas scrambled out of bed and tiptoed to the door in his nightshirt. Of course it had been Papa coming in the front door. He was probably having a mug of hot milk in his office right now, as he always did before bed. Now would be the perfect time to tell his news.

Everyone had turned in at ten o'clock as usual, and the

sounds of sleeping hummed at his ears as Thomas crept down
the back stairs to the dark hallway. He couldn't help but dart
uneasy glances into the shadows for the hooded man.

The door to the office was slightly ajar, and Thomas was
about to slip through it when the sound of his father's voice
stopped him. Who was in there with him at this hour?

Glancing down the blackened hallway, Thomas flattened
himself against the wall and listened.

"I have asked that You would spare me this walk," Papa
was saying. "But it seems You have other ideas for me."

Thomas chewed at his lip in the dark. Who on earth?
Who was higher than Papa, that he could have ideas for him?

"If I must face this, then please, Father, give me the
wisdom to do Your will. I know it isn't only my own freedom
that is at stake here."

Father? Thomas thought. *Daniel Hutchinson has been
dead since before I was born! How can Papa be talking to his
father?*

"I ask this in the name of Jesus Christ. Amen."

Amen? Thomas almost said out loud. That was what
Reverend Pendleton said at the end of the long prayers he
read from the book in church.

Had Papa been saying prayers that he made up out of his
head? Had he actually been talking to the spirit of his dead
father?

There was something familiar about what Papa had
said, Thomas thought as he leaned against the wall. *Please,
give me—*

Hadn't he himself said words like that . . . to someone?

I sure didn't think I was talking to Daniel Hutchinson! he
thought. Thomas shivered. It was time to go in and talk to

Papa, before he started seeing a ghost floating down the back stairs. Or a skeleton.

Thomas crept toward the door. But as he peeked inside, ready to speak to his father, he stopped again.

Papa was sitting at his desk, his hands folded against his forehead, his elbows resting on the desktop. He seemed to be listening.

Thomas quickly scanned the room with startled eyes. Was there someone else in the room with Papa? It felt as if there were.

Without a sound, Thomas crept away from the doorway and padded back up to his room. He could feel his heart pattering inside him as fast as a frightened rabbit's.

Only he wasn't afraid. He knew he'd just seen something private and special.

I wish I had someone like that to talk to, he thought sadly. *I need someone now.*

Thomas slept long after his usual dawn wake-up and had to be poked awake by an impatient Esther.

"Otis had to bring in the wood for the breakfast fire," Esther said as she whipped off his covers. "You'd think you were Governor Jefferson himself lyin' a-bed half the day."

"I'm coming," Thomas said, sailing for the basin on its stand in the corner. "But I have to talk to Papa first."

"You'll be hard put to do that. He's halfway to Hutchinson Homestead by now."

Thomas pulled his face out of the bowl. "No!" he cried.

"What are you caterwaulin' at me for?" Esther said. "He was up before dawn, tellin' your mother Clayton was a-goin' to need him."

"When will he be back?"

"By dark tonight. He said it never takes long to set those Ludwells straight."

Thomas nodded absently. He'd tell Papa about Alexander the minute he walked in the door.

"I'll be right down to do my chores," Thomas said.

"It's practically mid-morning. You'll be late for your lessons with Master Alexander if you don't shake a leg. He'll be here any minute."

She clucked off down the hall, and Thomas sank onto his bed with his shirt in his hand. Of course he would have to go on with his lessons as if nothing had happened until he had a chance to talk to Papa. Still, it was hard to believe that Alexander could be a Loyalist. He seemed to care about freedom.

Well, what do you think, Thomas? Sam would have said in disgust. *Do you think he's a spy?*

Thomas leaped from the bed so fast that he sent the covers flying off like a flock of startled geese. A spy! That had to be why Papa didn't know he'd hired a Loyalist. With all the important things Papa was doing in his office, Alexander probably thought he could gather information to give to the enemy—the Tories—maybe even the British themselves.

Thomas yanked a pair of breeches out of his clothes press and hopped on one foot to get them on. *There's really only one thing to do until Papa gets back*, he thought, *and that's keep an eye on Master Alexander Taylor.*

All morning, Thomas did ciphering problems and recited his Greek alphabet . . . and watched Alexander's every move. The most suspicious thing Thomas saw him do was peer into

Papa's inkwell while Thomas was searching for the West Indies on the globe.

He always does funny things like that, Thomas thought. But he made a mental note of it.

Poking around in Papa's things.

As much as he hoped he was helping his father, it was lonely work.

There was an empty hole where thoughts of afternoon adventures with Caroline usually bubbled and overflowed. And soon there would be another one where his lively question-and-answer sessions with Alexander lived.

I was alone when I came here, he told himself sternly as he rounded the corner of Gloucester that afternoon on his way to the apothecary shop. *So what's the difference now?*

"Well, see who's here, looking like he lost his best friend!"

Thomas's head jerked up from the sidewalk, and his gaze locked with the stony eyes of Henry Gates.

Chapter Eighteen

Fear flickered through Thomas. He hadn't seen Henry since the day he'd stolen Caroline's basket.

"What's wrong, Hutchinson?" Henry sneered. He crossed his dangly arms across his chest. "Cat got your tongue?"

Thomas stiffened and started to move past him, but Henry blocked his path. Thomas's neck began to sting.

"I know you're probably mad at me," Henry said. "It's true I've been making myself scarce, but it couldn't be helped. My father and I had . . . business to attend to."

Henry's thin lips split into a slit of a smile as he propped his elbow on the horse rail.

"So say something," he said.

"I don't have anything to say," Thomas told him stiffly. "I have to go or I'll be late for work."

"You'll want to hear what I have to say, though."

"What is it?"

Henry leaned back on his heels. Thomas glanced around him toward the apothecary shop, still 10 doors down.

"My father and I heard tell that up in New England, they string up Loyalists and poke fun at them, right on the streets," Henry said.

Thomas's eyes whipped to Henry's face. "We don't do that in Virginia."

"We do now."

"Where?"

"Out Petersburg way. My father knows how to get the Patriots going!"

Thomas's anger buzzed like a wasps' nest. "Don't be thinking you can try that here."

"Why? Because your father won't allow it? Ha! Let him try to stop us. We took apart one Tory farmer's wagon and put it back together on top of his chimney—and he never knew until the next morning!"

Henry's disturbing mouth broke open into a laugh, but Thomas stood as still as the horse post and glared at him.

"Was it you and your father who threw a rock through Robert Taylor's window yesterday?"

"What is that to you?" Henry said. "They're dirty Loyalists."

The anger pumped so hard up the back of Thomas's neck that he thought it would burst open. He clenched his fists.

But just as if Papa himself had been striding toward him down the sidewalk, he could almost hear him saying, *Have you ever known me to settle my differences with a brawl?*

"I'm going to work," Thomas said abruptly.

Henry stepped in his path once more, this time looking back over his shoulder in the direction of the shop.

"Go, then. Who's stopping you?"

"Certainly not you," Thomas said.

He twisted his shoulder to get past Henry without touching him and pounded up Duke of Gloucester Street.

You're the one who ought to be strung up on the street, Henry Gates, he thought fiercely. *You and your lying father.*

By the time Thomas reached the front door of the shop, he had been holding back his anger so tightly that he was certain he would snap off old Francis's nose if he said one word about his being late.

But the shop was empty when he opened the door. Strangely empty . . . as if Francis had suddenly dropped what he was doing and ran.

Thomas hurried inside. The small fire Francis kept going to heat ingredients was little more than a flicker, and his mortar and pestle were out on the counter, still filled with a half mixed paste. A trail of white powder led all the way across the counter onto the floor.

That wasn't like Francis at all. The man's whole head went crimson if Thomas left so much as a snippet of string lying about.

With a chill crawling uneasily up his spine, Thomas made his way slowly into the examination room.

"Francis?" Thomas said cautiously. "Mr. Pickering, where are you?"

From below, he heard a groan. Thomas's body turned to frost as he listened.

There was another moan. More pained this time, and wheezing out—

It was Francis! Thomas's feet unstuck from the floor, and he plowed toward the cellar steps. He stumbled down into the darkness, still calling, "Francis?"

He was answered with a groan from the far corner. Thomas stuck his hands out in front of him and charged toward the sound, jamming his thigh into a table edge.

Francis moaned again, and Thomas went down on his hands and knees and crawled to him. By now his eyes were getting used to the dim light, but it was his fingers that found the worst of it. There were thick ropes wrapped tightly all around the old man.

"Master Pickering!" Thomas cried. He felt for Francis's face and this time found a rag stuffed into his mouth. With trembling fingers, Thomas yanked it out and put his hand near Francis's lips to feel his breath.

It was there. He was alive . . . and still moaning.

"Francis," Thomas said very close to his ear. "Can you hear me? It's Thomas Hutchinson."

There was only a leaden silence.

Spirits of ammonia, Thomas thought.

Thomas tugged at the ropes and got them off. He tossed them aside as he banged and crashed his way to the stairs and tore up them, grabbing the candle out of its holder on the wall on the way.

Blanket. Spirits of ammonia. A light to see by.

Thomas tried to focus on those three things and keep the rest of the frightening voices back in a corner of his mind.

He pulled a blanket from the cabinet in the examination room and flopped it onto his shoulder. The spirits of ammonia were easy to find, and he tucked the bottle under his arm while he stuck the candle into the dwindling fire. Holding the candle in one hand, he tossed a log into the fireplace with the other. Francis was going to need to be warmed—if Thomas could get him up the stairs.

Shielding the flame with his hand, Thomas went back down into the cellar and stumbled his way to the corner. In the glow of the flame, he could clearly see the apothecary crumpled on the stone floor. Thomas gasped, nearly letting the medicine bottle crash at his feet.

The old man's face was smeared with blood, and his jaw was already swollen. His skin was the color of ash.

But he's still breathing, Thomas told himself as Francis's chest rattled through the cellar. Thomas poked the candle into a nearby holder and lifted Francis's head in the cradle of his arm.

"Just breathe this in," Thomas said as he held the bottle under Francis's nose. "Just breathe this in, and you'll cough right back to life."

At first there was nothing but a few feeble wheezes.

"Please," Thomas said. "Whoever that was my father was talking to, listen to me, too. Please, don't let him die."

He shoved the bottle practically up one of old Francis's nostrils, and with a shuddering gasp the old man's eyes flew open and he struggled to sit up.

"You're all right!" Thomas cried. "It's me—Hutchinson!"

Francis gave another raspy cough and squinted up at Thomas's face.

"Spec-tacles," he managed to get out.

Thomas glanced around, and his heart sank. Beneath the table was a tiny pile of smashed glass and a twisted gold frame.

"They're broken, sir," Thomas said. "I can help you up the stairs, though. I'm your eyes sometimes anyway. Here, take hold of my arm."

Francis fumbled for Thomas's sleeve and clutched at it as Thomas slowly drew him upward. But the groan that came out of him was his worst yet, and his face went white.

"Lay me back down!" Francis said. "They got me a good one in the stomach. I think something's amiss."

Thomas pushed down the panic inside him and stood up. "We need help," he said. "I'll fetch some. You stay here."

Francis groaned. "I'll not be going anywhere soon."

Thomas was up the stairs in two steps and out the front door in another three. The street, a snowstorm of spring blossoms, looked desolate and empty to Thomas's terrified eyes.

He flung himself down the front steps and craned his neck desperately up the Duke of Gloucester Street.

The door to the milliner's opened and a small figure stepped out. When Caroline saw him, she started to toss her head and look the other way, but her brown eyes seemed to hook on Thomas. They softened like pats of butter.

"Tom, what is it?" she said. "You're white as cream."

"It's Francis!" Thomas cried. "He was beaten and tied up in the cellar. I'm afraid he'll die! I need help, please!"

"One of our servants is at the silversmith's," she said. "I'll have him run and fetch Papa!"

Thomas fled back to the shop, and as he went, some of the fear that had squeezed his stomach let loose of its hold. It was always better when Caroline was there.

When they reached the cellar together, Francis was cold and still again.

"Slap his hands!" Thomas said.

Caroline went after Francis's clawlike palms while Thomas stuffed the spirits of ammonia under his nose. Once more, the old man sputtered back to them.

"Look at all this," Caroline whispered.

Thomas looked at the old, withered hand she was holding and bit his lip. Blood was gushing from a cut across his wrist.

"Is there any salt petre down here, sir?" Thomas said.

"Second drawer down," Francis said. "You can make a—"

"I'll make a poultice," Thomas said, "and then pack it with salt of ammonia."

Within minutes, Thomas had Francis's hand cleaned and packed and was wrapping it in a piece of cloth from Caroline's petticoat.

"Must've happened when they shoved me against the table," Francis said.

"Who shoved you?" Thomas asked.

"Two men. I couldn't see who they were. They were wearing black hoods over their heads and faces."

Thomas stopped wrapping. "Black hoods?"

Francis closed his eyes. "I know. You told me there was a man in a black hood in here yesterday, and I didn't believe you. He must have slipped in the side door to take me then, but a customer came in, I suppose. Bloody thieves, they were."

"Monsters," said Caroline. "Can I fetch you some water, Mr. Pickering?"

Francis nodded, and Caroline scurried off. "I'll watch for Papa," she whispered to Thomas.

"What did these men want?" Thomas said.

"They didn't do me the courtesy of telling me," Francis said, wincing. "The taller one used some kind of disguised voice to tell me they were Loyalists. Who else would it be? It's sure they were after some of my goods. You check for me, Hutchinson. You know what's there."

"I will," Thomas said solemnly.

"They didn't say much else to me, which leads me to believe they were afraid I'd recognize them." Francis fought for his next breath. "I did hear the shorter one whisper to the other to hurry up and tie me because 'he' would be along any minute. The taller one told him to go on and head 'him' off." The old man moaned, and Thomas could see him slipping away again. "Who is that girl with you?"

"She's Ca—"

Thomas caught himself. There was no one old Francis disliked more than a Loyalist, and Thomas had one heading here right now to rescue them. He swallowed hard.

"She's a friend," he said.

"This is brave of you, Hutchinson. I know how frightened you are of coming down to the cellar, though heaven knows why."

He floated off again, and Thomas stared at him for a moment before he tucked the blanket up under his chin.

So he knew all along I was afraid. That's why he never made me come down here.

"He's here, Tom!" Caroline called from the stairs.

With a clatter of footsteps, she and her father were at Francis's side. Robert Taylor ran his serious eyes over the old apothecary and looked at Thomas.

"You're the expert, son," he said. "What should we do?"

Thomas shook his head. "Let's take him up by the fire."

Caroline's father climbed the stairs with Francis in his arms while Caroline arranged a bed in front of the fireplace and Thomas stoked the fire. Francis began to breathe easier, but his face was as gray as his hair.

"He seems to be resting better now," Mr. Taylor said. "He'll need nursing, though."

Thomas nodded, but his mind was roaming around the shop.

Were those men in the black hoods just here to hurt Francis, or did they steal something? Surely not money. Francis never keeps any here. He says no one ever pays their bills.

And then he saw it. The glass-fronted cabinet was empty. The jar of gold powder was gone.

With a bolt that nearly knocked Caroline off her feet, Thomas rushed to Francis and peered under the blanket. There was no chain around his waist—and no key.

"Oh, no!" Thomas moaned.

"He's going to be all right, son," Mr. Taylor said softly. "Let's just let him sleep."

"What's to be done with him now, Papa?" Caroline said.

As they continued to whisper by the fireplace, Thomas went to the shop window and stared out. His reflection stared back at him . . . and it had all the answers.

It wasn't Loyalists at all. It was Henry Gates and his father, there to take—

Thomas looked back at the gold cabinet and cringed as if he'd been made a fool of in front of all of Bruton Parish Church.

Henry only tried to be my "partner" so he could find out where the gold powder was . . . and I told him.

Angry tears filled Thomas's eyes as he remembered that day—how he'd wanted to show Henry that he knew all about the shop, so he led him right to the gold, telling him where Francis kept the key and where there was even more gold.

With a cry, Thomas snatched up the candle and flew across the room and around the corner to the stairs. In the cellar, he held the candle high and searched the room.

There it was, another glass-fronted cabinet—empty.

Thomas's heart thudded to a stop inside him, and he began to lower the candle. His hand hit on something, and it swung crazily above his head.

With a gasp, Thomas jumped back. In his haste, he'd forgotten about the bodies left hanging from the ceiling to rot away into skeletons.

But he blinked and held the candle up again.

"Those aren't bodies!" he said to the empty cellar. "Those are herbs drying!"

Thomas shook his head and trudged back up the stairs.

I thought I was actually on my way to being as smart as Papa and the others, he said to himself. *But I'm as big an oaf as I ever was.*

Thomas leaned heavily against the wall of the stairwell. Francis had said, "You have no idea what I will do to you if any harm comes to this gold at your hands." But that wasn't what was crushing Thomas's chest. *I let them take all of Francis's gold and nearly kill him*, he thought. *I deserve to be turned into a skeleton.*

"Don't worry, Tom," said a soft voice at the top of the stairs. "Papa says he thinks the old man will be all right."

Thomas slid down against the wall of the hallway and sat on the floor, his shoulders drooping as low as his spirits. Caroline lowered herself beside him and sat with her pink-flowered skirt puffed around her.

"Really, he will," Caroline said. "Papa has sent for our carriage, and we're going to take Mr. Pickering to our house until he's well."

Thomas shook his head. "It isn't just that. This whole thing is my fault."

"How can you say that?"

"Because it's true."

"Tom, really—"

"You don't understand!"

"Then tell me."

They were doing it again, throwing words back and forth like angry balls. But when Thomas looked up at Caroline, she didn't seem angry at all. Her brown eyes were wide and her dimples were deep, as if she cared more about what kind of trouble Thomas was in than she did about anything else.

Thomas sighed, and then he told her everything, from the first day Henry Gates had walked into the shop until today when he'd found Francis unconscious in the cellar.

"See?" he said when he was finished. "It's my fault."

Caroline sat up straight and smoothed her skirt thoughtfully over her knees.

"Well, then," she said, "we'll just have to fix it."

"Fix it? How?"

"I don't know," she said cheerfully. "But we'll think of something. We always do."

For a moment, Thomas felt a glimmer of hope flickering to life somewhere inside him. After all, he and Caroline were partners.

But then another thought came along and snuffed it out.

We aren't partners anymore. She's a Loyalist, and I'm a Patriot.

"I don't know," Thomas said. "You're a Loyalist and—"

Her wedge of a smile slid away from her face. For an awful instant, Thomas thought she was going to cry. But there was a step in the hall, and Robert Taylor's gentle voice said, "The carriage is here."

Caroline gathered herself up and hurried after her father without a backward glance. Thomas fought back his own tears and followed her.

✛ ✛ ✛

Chapter Nineteen

There was only one thing to do now, Thomas decided at supper that night as he toyed with the cornbread on his plate. He hadn't told anyone about Francis yet, but as soon as Papa came home from Hutchinson Homestead, he was going to tell him everything—about Henry Gates and about Alexander, and even about his friendship with Caroline.

He'll give up on me, I know, Thomas thought miserably. *But people are getting hurt now, and more people might. And it's because of me.*

Just then the door swung open and Papa's square shoulders filled its frame. His face was pinched and white.

"John!" Mama cried. "What is it? What's happened?"

Papa shook his head. "It has not been a happy journey. I fear the Ludwells have my head in a noose this time."

Thomas saw the same fear flash across Mama's face that he felt in his chest. "But how can that be?" she said.

"It seems that Carter Ludwell has accused Clayton, and thus me, of setting traps for his cows. He's found several of them dead at the edge of his land that is next to ours. One of our own servants claims he saw Clayton set the traps in the dead of night, about a week ago."

"Why, that's impossible!"

"Of course, it is. With the trouble he has walking and his weak heart, Clayton never ventures to the far reaches of the property."

Mama's face drained, and she leaned in to put her arm on Papa's sleeve. "Surely the court will see that Clayton couldn't possibly do such a thing."

"That is my hope," Papa said. "This is indeed a matter for the General Court, but they don't meet for three months."

Mama patted his arm. "That's plenty of time for the truth to come to light."

"And plenty of time for Clayton and I to sit in jail," Papa said darkly.

Thomas could hold back his fury no longer. "They won't listen to Ludwell!" he burst out. "He's a Loyalist!"

Papa looked startled, then slowly shook his head.

"I'm afraid I've dug my own grave, Thomas," he said. "And perhaps Clayton's, too. I am the one who has insisted that it be a policy in Williamsburg that Loyalists be treated like everyone else." He gripped his lips together in a sad smile. "I can't bend the rules now to suit myself."

Mama's gray eyes were shining with tears in the candlelight. "What will you do, John?" she said.

"Pray," he said simply. "Right here, with my family."

Mama nodded and bowed her head, and Papa folded his hand over hers as he did the same. Obediently, Thomas bent his head and closed his eyes, but he knew something very different was about to happen.

"Father," Papa said, "we come to You with heavy hearts."

Thomas couldn't stop himself from chancing a glance at his father. Was he talking to Daniel Hutchinson again? Did Mama know about this?

"We pray that not only will You give the magistrates the wisdom to see that justice is done, but that You will enter the heart of Carter Ludwell, oh, God, and direct it in the way of truth and peace. . . ."

God? Thomas thought. *The God in the prayer book? The God Reverend Pendleton talks about in his sermons? That's who Papa is talking to? He's asking for help as if He were right here, just like I ask . . . someone—*

"In the name of Your son, our savior, Jesus Christ. Amen."

Thomas opened one eye and peeked at his father. There was a look of peace on his tired face.

"I feel strengthened," Papa said. "I know what I have to do." He stood up. "I shall be in my office most of the night," he said. "I hope you two will rest well."

So once again there was no chance to talk to Papa about Alexander or anything else. But someone had to know about Francis, and before he went to bed, Thomas went to the parlor where Mama sat with her sewing and told her how he'd found the old apothecary in the cellar, how his gold powder had been stolen, and how Robert Taylor had taken him home. He left out the details about his "friendship" with Henry—and Caroline.

When he stopped, Mama said, "We can do something about this. I must have Esther make some special soup—"

"We want Mr. Pickering to get *well*, Mama!" Thomas said.

She laughed her bell-laugh. "And you must be the one to take it to him, Thomas. You probably saved his life!"

"But the Taylors are Loyalists. Won't that look bad for Papa?"

Mama knitted her delicate eyebrows together. "I am so tired of worrying about what looks bad," she said. "When can we get back to wondering what looks right to God?"

There He was again, Thomas thought. He looked side-ways at his mother. "Do you *talk* to God? I mean, the way Papa did tonight?"

She arched her eyebrows at him. "If you mean do I pray, yes."

"But I thought praying was out of the prayer book."

Mama put her sewing aside and leaned forward to look into his eyes.

"Praying from the book is one way," she said. "It's familiar and beautiful. But there are times when we need to talk to God personally, and then we have to make up our own prayers. Your father is very good at it."

"How do *you* talk to God?" Thomas said.

"Well, I simply say, 'Father, please . . .' and then whatever it is I need. I prayed hard when we first came to Williamsburg and you were so unhappy. And He answered me, at least for a while. Now you seem sad again, but I suppose you're worried about old Mr. Pickering and about Papa and Clayton. But talk to God, Thomas. He'll help you."

Thomas said good-night to his mother and went up to bed. He propped up on one elbow and looked out at the velvet sky.

"God?" he said uncertainly. "If You're listening, please help me. I have to prove that Henry Gates took the gold . . . and tell Papa that Alexander is a Loyalist . . . and I want to keep Caroline for my friend . . . and Alexander for my teacher . . . and please keep Clayton and Papa out of jail."

He was sure God had a head full by now, with all three Hutchinsons praying, so he hunkered down under the covers.

But he sat up once again and said, "Amen."

☨ ⁜ ☨

Chapter Twenty

homas was on his way to North England Street in the pink glow of early morning with a jar of Esther's soup. *Please, God*, he prayed clumsily. *Don't let me see Caroline.*

When the Taylors' front door opened, it was Alexander whose bright face greeted him.

"Here's our hero!" he said, dimples flashing in his cheeks.

Thomas shrugged and thrust the jar of soup into Alexander's hands.

"This is for Mr. Pickering," he said. "It's probably awful. Esther made it."

Alexander nodded with a twinkle in his honey-brown eyes. "I know Mr. Pickering would like to see you. Will you come up?"

Before Thomas could answer, Alexander was ushering him up the U-shaped staircase to a wood-paneled room. He could barely see Francis's face in the midst of all the cushions and velvety red bed hangings.

"There's someone here to see you, sir," Alexander whispered toward the pile of pillows. The faded eyes fluttered open and rested on Thomas.

"Hello, sir." Thomas had to bite his lip to keep from blurting out, "Look what they've done to you!"

The withered face was black and purple and swollen, and his bandaged wrist lay limp on the pillow like a broken bird's wing.

Thomas could feel his heart breaking.

"Sir?" he said. "Those men . . . they took your gold."

"I know." Francis paused while his breath rattled, and Thomas swallowed hard against his tears. "Stole my key, they did. But you . . . you're not to be in that shop alone—"

"I'm sorry," Thomas said.

"—they may come back and hurt you, too. Help young Taylor here. Show him . . . "

"Show him what?" Thomas asked.

But Francis only sighed and drifted off again.

"His body needs the sleep," Alexander said at Thomas's elbow. "The old fellow's been through a great deal."

"What was he talking about?" Thomas asked. "What am I supposed to help you with?"

Alexander said, "I don't think the old man's totally in his right mind yet. He asked me to keep an eye on his shop until he's able to return."

"You!"

Alexander laughed nervously. "That was my reaction, too. What do I know about an apothecary shop?"

Not only that, Thomas almost shouted, *but you're a Loyalist. Francis Pickering hates Loyalists!*

"I'll ask your father if we can do your lessons at the shop in the mornings," Alexander was saying. "That way I can keep an eye on things, and you can show me what to do."

"My father isn't at home this morning," Thomas said.

"Old Francis wants you protected. Do you think your papa will mind?"

When he finds out you're a Loyalist, yes! Thomas wanted to answer. But he shook his head.

"Good, then. Shall we meet there in an hour?"

Thomas nodded and backed toward the door. This was all too confusing.

"Sir?" Alexander was whispering to Francis. "Would you care for some breakfast?"

"Where's the girl?" Francis muttered. "Can you have her bring it to me?"

"Certainly."

Alexander turned to Thomas. "Caroline is lurking out in the hall. Would you poke your head out and tell her to bring Mr. Pickering's breakfast up?"

Thomas darted out into the hall. *If I can get out of here fast enough*, he thought, *there's a good chance Mr. Pickering will get no breakfast at all!*

But as soon as the bedroom door shut behind him, a figure in a blue linen dress slipped out from behind the tall case clock in the hall.

"Get Francis's breakfast," he said before she could speak.

Thomas took off down the hall, but he knew he had Caroline right on his heels.

"If you're sure Henry Gates and his father took the old man's gold, you'll have to prove it," she called after him.

Thomas stopped so fast that she plowed into the back of him.

"How?" he said without turning to look at her.

"I think you should sneak into his house and search for the evidence."

"What?"

Thomas whirled to face her. Her eyes were already full of plans.

"I could help you," she said. "We're smart enough. We've come up with far more complicated schemes than that just playing on the bridge." Her brown eyes grew shiny. "This will be much more fun."

"But it isn't right," Thomas said.

Caroline put her hands on her hips. "Was it right for Henry Gates and his evil father to do what they did?"

"No, but—"

"Then there you have it, don't you?" Caroline primly tucked her hair into her cap. "You'll simply slip in through a window while I make sure no one catches you."

"*I'll* sneak through a window?"

"That should work fine, but I'll take Martha along just in case."

Thomas's stomach was juggling his breakfast. "We don't even know where they live!"

"I found out—Number Two Queen Street."

"How . . . ?" Then Thomas shook the plan out of his head, where it had already begun to take hold. "No. We can't be partners anymore. I told you."

"Just because I come from a Loyalist family?" she said, eyes narrowing. "You know, I've been thinking about this since yesterday. It didn't bother Francis Pickering to take help from Loyalists. I don't know what makes you so much better, Tom Hutchinson!"

She gathered up the blue linen and flounced past him. "You just wait," she said over her shoulder. "You'll find out you need my help."

All through his chores, Thomas's mind did somersaults. One minute it seemed that everything Sam had told him about not being friends with a Loyalist seemed right. But the next minute, Caroline's warning that she needed his help was making sense. By the time he headed for the apothecary shop, he was thinking about what Caroline said—about sneaking into Henry's house. *I won't do it*, he thought, as he crossed the Duke of Gloucester Street. *I'll just look at it*. That was how he ended up standing in front of Number Two Queen Street. But he wasn't at all sure how Caroline got there.

"So you changed your mind then?" she asked from behind him.

Thomas jumped clumsily. "You shouldn't sneak up on people like that!"

"And you shouldn't be so easy to follow."

She leaned her elbow on the covered basket she was carrying. "So are you going to do it?"

"What?"

"Go in Henry's house."

Thomas rolled his eyes. "This isn't a game, Caroline."

She planted her hands on her hips. "I know that, Tom. But you don't have to climb through a window. You can pretend to be calling on him, and while you're talking, I can get his attention so you can look around—"

"—to see if I can spot the black hoods and the key," he finished for her.

Caroline nodded and smiled eagerly. Thomas juggled his thoughts again. If he went into Henry Gates's house and was caught, he'd have to face Papa like a thief. He'd be packed off to the Homestead or worse. But if he didn't do this, Henry and his father might get away—with old Francis lying there in that bed with his head all lumpy and swelled up.

And then another thought entered, uninvited. *When will you think about someone besides yourself?* it said. Thomas put his face in his hands for a minute. *Please, God. Help me know which thought to listen to.*

"Tom?" Caroline said.

"All right, then," he said. "What excuse shall I use for calling on him?"

The Gates's house was a narrow one, only one room wide, painted the color of Esther's cooked turnips. The garden in front was choked with weeds, and Thomas tripped on a loose stone in the walkway as they went toward the front door.

"Oaf," Caroline whispered, and grinned at him.

Henry met them at the front door before Thomas could knock, his wide mouth opened in a suspicious slit. "What do you want?" he said. "I thought you'd decided you were too good for me, Hutchinson."

"He's come to apologize," Caroline said. She gave Thomas a shove forward. "May we come in?"

Henry stared at her as she pranced past him into the dark front hall, carrying her basket.

"What is she doing here?" Henry said to Thomas.

"I've brought you some sugar muffins as a peace offering." She swung the basket forward. As she did, the cover came off. There was a sudden burst of orange fur and claws—and Caroline held it close to Henry's face.

"No!" Henry shrieked.

"Why, Martha!" Caroline said merrily. "I had no idea you were in there!"

"I hate this cat!"

Caroline's eyes twinkled as Martha continued to snarl and

smack at Henry's face with her paw. "How rude, Henry," she said. "You'll hurt her feelings!"

"Get her away from me!" cried Henry.

Caroline shot Thomas a look that said, "Now's your chance. Start searching!"

Thomas nodded and backed silently toward the crooked little staircase that led to the second floor. At the same time, Caroline turned Martha loose. In a flash, the cat was tensed up to spring at Henry again. Henry bolted into the dining room with a stiff-haired Martha hissing behind him.

Thomas climbed the stairs three at a time and found himself in a hall that was as black as soot even in the mid-morning. He felt his way along a dusty wall of peeling wallpaper until he found a doorway. The door squeaked as he let himself in, but he knew Henry would never hear it—not the way he was carrying on down below.

Some sunlight did manage to struggle through the room's dirty gray window, and Thomas could make out a lumpy pallet on the floor and a pile of what looked like rags—and smelled like them, too. Thomas gave the mound of smelly cloth another disgusted look. But his eyes hooked on something black, something that looked sinister in the midst of the homespun shirts.

"Martha, kitty, kitty!" Thomas heard Caroline call out a little too loudly from beneath him. "Don't go upstairs!"

He had run out of time. Heart battering at his chest, Thomas snatched up the black thing and stuffed it under his shirt. From out of its folds, a vial fell. The gold. Thomas scooped it up and tucked it in with the hood. Yanking his vest tightly around him, he plunged out of the room and down the steps. At the bottom, Martha zipped across his path, followed by a red-faced Henry. Caroline brought up the rear and stopped in front of Thomas.

"I'll grab Martha on the next pass," she said cheerfully. "You go on ahead, and I'll meet you by the Capitol Building. Nobody will see us there. No one goes there anymore."

Thomas nodded and went for the door. He noticed Henry approaching, with his teeth clenched and eyes narrowed into slits.

Caroline leaned close to Thomas and whispered, "You got it, didn't you?"

Thomas grinned. Then he slid out the door and into the sunlight.

Caroline caught up to him under a big live oak tree in front of the deserted Capitol Building, out of breath but already talking.

"Now you can go to your father, Tom," she said. "You have all the proof you need."

Her brown eyes were shining, and she swung the cat basket at her side.

"Why are you so happy about this?" Thomas said. "I mean, old Francis is nothing to you."

She arched her almost invisible eyebrows. "How do you know? Have you been in my house since Papa brought him there yesterday? Did you watch while I fed him his supper with a spoon? Did you see him smile when I put the bouquet of daffodils next to his bed?"

Thomas looked down at his shoe buckles. "All of that happened?"

"Yes."

Thomas flounced down on the grass and frowned. "I don't

understand it. Henry Gates is the meanest person I ever knew, but he's a Patriot, so he's on our side. You and Alexander and your mother and father do things for people—but you're Loyalists and I'm supposed to stay away from you. When my father finds out Alexander is a Loyalist, I know he won't let him teach me anymore. But it's Alexander who is minding Francis's apothecary shop. I don't understand!"

Caroline shook her head. "I don't either. It seems so silly to me." She poked him gently with her foot. "You'd better hide. There's a wagon coming."

Thomas scrambled up to a low branch on the live oak and watched the wagon that lumbered toward them. There was something different about it. The man who drove the sad-looking horses was wearing a black three-cornered hat as if he were someone important. Thomas's eyes sprang open.

"That's Peter Pelham!" he whispered hoarsely. "He's the jailer!"

"They must be going to lock someone up, then. Can you see who it is?"

Thomas stood up on the branch and stretched. His heart thudded to a stop in his chest, and his words came out in a whimper. "Caroline! It's my father!"

✦ ✦ ✦

Chapter Twenty-One

Thomas dropped from the tree and hurled himself after the wagon.

"Tom! No!" Caroline cried. "What are you doing?"

"That's Papa! They're taking him away!"

Anger burned up the back of Thomas's neck as he dug his feet into the muddy road and tore after the wagon shouting, "Stop! Stop, I say!"

Peter Pelham didn't stop. In fact, he seemed to spur the bony horses on faster. A man in a dark-blue cape who sat next to Papa kept his back to Thomas.

As the wagon bounced and jostled on the rutted road toward the jail, Thomas ran after it, his hands in tight balls at his sides.

"Why don't you stop?" he shouted again.

This time, the man in the dark-blue cape leaned over the back of the wagon. Thomas's fury doubled when he saw that it was Xavier Wormeley, the magistrate.

"Go away now, boy," Xavier said. "This is official business. It has nothing to do with you."

"It does! That's my father!"

Xavier only waved Thomas off with his sausage fingers and settled himself back into the wagon.

And then it was as if a giant, angry hand took hold of Thomas from behind and shoved him forward. It didn't feel like his own feet that carried him to the front of the wagon and planted him right in the path of the oncoming horses.

"Whoa!" Peter Pelham called to them. He pulled the team to a stop.

Wormeley climbed from the wagon and stalked toward him. Thomas flew at him with his fists pounding the air. He felt one hit Xavier's soft jowls.

"Ow!" cried Wormeley. "Peter, help me!"

Thomas kept struggling and kicking and shouting until two arms came around him from behind like iron bands. Even then, he only quit flailing when he heard his father's voice cry, "Thomas! Stop at once!"

Thomas stiffened like a post.

"What do you mean by this, boy?" Mr. Wormeley cried. "I could have you jailed for this!"

"Don't be a fool, Xavier," John Hutchinson said from the wagon. "He's my son. It was only natural for him to try to protect me. Let go of him, I beg you."

Xavier's jowls trembled. "Only if you call him off, John. I won't be pummeled like a common slave."

"Thomas," Papa said sternly. "When this man turns you loose, you are to go home at once, do you hear? You can help me by making no more trouble. We will have justice, I promise you."

Inside his chest, Thomas felt his heart cracking in two. He only wanted to help, but Papa had said it himself—he was only making more trouble.

"Yes, sir," he said miserably.

"You heard the boy, Xavier," Papa said. "Let him go."

Xavier Wormeley gave one more shake of his jowls before
he nodded importantly to Peter Pelham, and Thomas was
tumbled to the ground.

He couldn't look at his father as he picked himself up and
stood off to the side of the road. He only lifted his eyes when
the wagon made the last curve toward the jail, and then they
were filled with hot, angry tears.

"What's happened, Tom?" said a soft voice behind him.
"What has your father done?"

"He hasn't done anything!" Thomas cried. He whirled on
Caroline with his fists doubled.

She didn't even flinch, and Thomas let them fall helplessly to his sides.

"Carter Ludwell is a lousy Loyalist, and he has accused
Clayton and Papa of killing his cows. But they didn't do it.
They didn't!"

"Of course he didn't," Caroline said. "Carter Ludwell is a
thief and a swindler."

Thomas smeared his nose with his sleeve and stared at
her. "You know Carter Ludwell?"

"My father does. They grew up together. Papa always says
those things about him—and that he's a coward. Papa could
always run him off when he bullied the other boys."

"I'm a coward, too," Thomas said. He smashed at his
tears angrily with his fists.

"You are no such thing! What are you going to do?"

"Papa told me to go home."

"I know what he told you, Tom, but what are you going to
do? Let him sit in jail?"

Thomas's face jerked up. There was a twinkle in
Caroline's eye. "No!" he said.

"All right, then. I think we should go see my father."

"*Your* father?"

"He's just as good a man as yours, Tom Hutchinson, and I'll prove it to you!"

In a flurry of skirts and mob cap and basketful of cat, Caroline took off toward Nicholson Street. Thomas knew he had no choice but to follow her.

Robert Taylor was sitting at his desk in his polished study with a quill pen in his hand when Caroline burst in with Thomas behind her.

"Caroline, my dear," he said kindly. "I'm working."

"I'm sorry, Papa," Caroline said breathlessly, "but you have to help Thomas's father."

Mr. Taylor looked uncertainly at Thomas. "What kind of trouble is he in?"

In a rush of tangled words, Caroline poured out the story of Carter Ludwell's accusation. When she was finished, she rocked back on her heels and glanced over her shoulder at Thomas as if to say, "I told you so."

Robert Taylor rearranged a few things on his desk and finally looked up at his daughter.

"My dear," he said. "I hate to see any man accused unjustly. But I don't see what I can possibly do. I am a Loyalist. If I make trouble—"

"You helped Francis!" she cried.

"I didn't have to become involved with the law in order to do it," he said. "Opening my home to an injured old man is not the same as standing toe to toe with Xavier Wormeley."

"That mean old swine!"

"Caroline!" her father said sharply.

"Never mind, Caroline," Thomas said.

They both looked at him as if they had forgotten he was there.

"I knew he wouldn't help my father." Thomas could feel his voice pinching—and his heart breaking open even wider. "It's just like Sam says. You can't trust a Loyalist to help you."

"Son—" Robert Taylor started to say.

But his words were cut short by a furious banging in the direction of the front door.

"What on earth?" he said. He went to the window and slanted the blinds open. Thomas saw his face grow stiff.

"It's Xavier Wormeley," he said. "He has Gates and the boy with him."

Before he could get to the door of his study, it was flung open. A pale Betsy Taylor fluttered her hands and said, "I'm sorry, Robert. They forced their way past me."

"It's all right," Robert Taylor said. "I'll handle this. Caroline, you and Thomas run on now."

"No!" Xavier Wormeley cried out, waving his cape for effect. "This girl is precisely the one I want." He narrowed his poke-hole eyes, first at Caroline and then at her father. "I knew you Loyalists couldn't keep from making trouble for much longer, but I had no idea it would be your 10-year-old daughter who would make the first move."

"I demand to know what you're talking about," Robert Taylor said. He drew himself up in front of Xavier Wormeley until Thomas thought he looked as tall as his own father.

Wormeley jabbed a finger toward Caroline. "Mr. Gates here came to me just a few minutes ago with his son. He claims that your daughter pushed her way into his house and attacked him."

Tall, skinny Mr. Gates stood beside a smirking Henry near the window and directed his musket-ball eyes at Mr. Taylor.

Robert Taylor sputtered. "My daughter—barely a bushel's worth of child—*attacked* this strapping boy?" He looked admiringly at Caroline. "My, my. I had no idea of your strength."

"This is no laughing matter!" Xavier Wormeley exploded his cape out to both sides. "Look at the scratch on his face."

"She came into my house and set her cat on me!" Henry cried.

Robert Taylor looked at Caroline. "Is this true?"

"Yes!" Caroline said cheerfully.

"I daresay you put her up to it as part of some master plan," Wormeley said.

"Don't be absurd!"

"I will not pursue this further, Mr. Taylor . . . *if* you will agree to leave Williamsburg at once."

Xavier gave a last sweeping look around the room and with a waft of his cape started for the door. For the second time that day, Thomas flung himself into the man's path.

"You again!" Xavier shrieked. "Don't you touch me, boy!"

"It wasn't Caroline's fault!" Thomas cried. "She only went to protect me from Henry Gates while I searched his room!"

"Searched my room?" Henry said.

"What were you thinking of?" he cried. The magistrate took hold of Thomas's arm.

"I was looking for evidence that it was he and his father who robbed Francis Pickering and beat him up," Thomas said, "and I found it!"

Yanking himself away from Xavier Wormeley, Thomas thrust his hand inside his shirt and pulled out the black hood and vial of gold. The entire room seemed to gasp at once as he spread them out on the polished wooden floor.

Xavier broke the silence by grabbing Thomas's arm again and pulling him close to his face. "You're a liar, young Hutchinson, just like your father! You used this hood yourself to attack Francis Pickering and steal this gold."

"Good heavens, man!" said Robert Taylor. "Why would he do such a thing?"

Xavier dropped Thomas's arm and swaggered across the room, jowls wobbling. He put a finger close to Robert Taylor's chest. "To give the gold to the British—through lying, thieving Loyalists like yourself." He whirled to face Thomas. "Your father put you up to it, didn't he? He is in a league with Mr. Taylor!" Xavier gave him a long look before he took Thomas's arm roughly once more. "I can't prove that yet, but so help me I will." He smiled at Mr. Gates and Henry. "You men may go home now and rest assured there will be no more trouble from the Loyalists or their sympathizers."

"Wormeley! Think, man!" Robert Taylor strode toward him, his face pale. "Why, then, are you accusing John Hutchinson of killing Loyalist Ludwell's cows if he's on the side of the Loyalists?"

Xavier tapped his own head with his finger. "I *have* thought, sir. Killing Ludwell's cows was just a way of making us think he's a true Patriot, but I was not fooled." Thomas winced as the sausage fingers dug into his flesh. "For now, the boy goes off to jail to join his father. I once more recommend that you begin packing, Mr. Taylor . . . before you are driven out of town without a thing to your name."

As Xavier hauled him out the study door, Thomas could only look over his shoulder and plead with his eyes. Caroline looked back from inside the fold of her father's arms, tears streaming down her cheeks.

By the time Peter Pelham slammed the wooden door with its iron hinges behind him, Thomas was shaking so hard even his teeth were knocking against each other. Plunged into darkness that was only broken by the checkerboard of bars at the tiny window, Thomas rolled with the shove the jailer gave him and curled up in a ball on the damp floor. Straw stuck into his cheek, and something chittered and ran across his hand. Thomas began to sob.

"Thomas?" said a voice out of the inky blackness.

Thomas couldn't answer, even when he felt strong arms come around him. It was only when he smelled a little bit of sweat, horse soap, and lilac water that he knew his father was holding him.

"Papa," Thomas sobbed. "I'm sorry."

His father held him out at arm's length and searched his face. "Sorry for what, Thomas? Tell me why they've brought you here."

Thomas hung his head in misery. *If I'm going to admit to Papa what I've done, I have to tell everything. He's going to be so disappointed in me. He might even send me back to the Homestead, away from Francis and Alexander and Caroline.*

Thomas sighed from the bottom of his soul. What did it matter now? He would probably never see any of them again anyway.

With the fading afternoon light straining to get through the barred window, Thomas told his father everything. Papa only grunted now and then. When he was finished, his father was silent, and Thomas's heart sank even further into the empty pit inside him.

Finally, Papa cleared his throat. "Thomas, I think we had better pray."

Thomas nodded and bowed his head. *I've been praying all day, and look where it's gotten me*, he thought.

His heart ached inside of him, broken into too many pieces to ever put back together. *It hurts, God*, was all he could pray.

The afternoon finally slid away into evening, and then the cell was so dark that Thomas couldn't see his father's face. Somewhere in the smothering blackness Thomas fell asleep with his head against his father's shoulder. He awoke drenched in sweat and crying.

"Hold on now, son," Papa was saying into his hair. "Just hold on to me and pray."

"I'm a coward, Papa," Thomas sobbed. "I thought I was such a . . . such a big bully . . . but I'm nothing but a coward."

Papa reached out and brushed a finger across a tear on Thomas's cheek. "A coward is someone who won't admit that he is wrong. You've been honest with me. That took great courage."

The words echoed in Thomas's head as if he'd heard them before, only from someone else. From Alexander Taylor—who thought just like Papa. Only he was a Loyalist.

"I hate Xavier Wormeley!" Thomas burst out.

"Those are strong words, Thomas."

"He comes into the apothecary shop every week, and I serve him. But on Sunday when you introduced him to me, he acted like he'd never seen me before, because he thought I was a lowly sort." Thomas doubled his fists. "We have to win this war so everyone can be the same and think what they want and have who they want as friends!"

John Hutchinson pulled Thomas up against him and held on. "Sleep now," he said in a husky voice. "You'll need your strength for whatever lies ahead."

Thomas drifted fitfully back to sleep, and among his dreams he heard his father talking softly, saying "Father" and "Amen." When he came fully awake, it was a surge of bright sunlight that brought him sitting straight up.

"Good morning, Mr. Hutchinson," said Peter Pelham. "I'm letting you go."

John Hutchinson sprang to his feet, and Thomas scrambled up beside him.

"We're to be released?"

Thomas could see Peter Pelham grinning now, all the way up to his ears.

"At the orders of the magistrate himself," the jailer announced. "You've both been cleared of the charges."

"How—?" Papa started to say. But he stopped and took Thomas by the arm. "Let's be on our way, Thomas. Before Mr. Wormeley changes his mind!"

Thomas had never smelled the cherry blossoms or heard the mockingbirds or seen the church spire cut against the sky as clearly as he did that morning as he and Papa fairly raced home. And never had his mother's bell voice sounded so sweet in his ear as she pulled him to her at the front door and then examined his every bone.

"Oh, my darlings," she said, trying to hug Thomas and her husband at the same time. "Was it terribly dreadful?"

"It was," Papa said. "But it's over. The question is, *why* is it over? I want to find out how this all became untangled."

Mama took his hands, and her pretty face grew serious. "I

know why and how and everything," she said. "And they're here in the parlor, waiting to tell you themselves."

"Who?" Papa asked.

"Please, John, don't be angry with me for letting them in. But after all they've done, I could hardly turn them away."

Just then the parlor door flew open, and Sam burst through with Clayton limping behind him at a more sedate pace.

"Father!" Sam cried.

And Clayton added, "Thank God!"

"I've been keeping an eye on them, sir," Sam said. "They did come forward on your behalf, and Thomas's. But I thought they bore watching."

Papa's eyebrows shot up to his hairline. "Who are these mystery people?"

Sam nodded his blond head toward the parlor, and Thomas crept forward to get a look.

There, standing in front of the fireplace, was Robert Taylor. And beside him was Caroline.

Chapter Twenty-Two

"Mr. Taylor," John Hutchinson said as he stepped into the parlor. "To what do I owe the honor, sir?" His voice was polite but cool, and Thomas couldn't look at Caroline. He didn't want to see her face when his father asked them just as politely to leave. His chest started to ache again.

Caroline's father nodded respectfully. "I only came to tell your wife that you would soon be released from the jail," he said. "But she insisted that I stay and tell you the story myself."

He looked quietly to Papa as if for approval, and Thomas saw his father nod. It struck him how much alike the two men were.

"After Thomas was taken off by Mr. Wormeley, Caroline was quite upset. Truly, I could not console her. I tell you, Mr. Hutchinson, I call myself a Loyalist, but I have never seen such loyalty to a friend as she displayed for your son. She insisted that if the Gates's house would only be searched, another black hood would be found and more gold and perhaps a key to Mr. Pickering's gold cabinets. Of course I was willing to see that that was done."

Mr. Taylor paused, and pain spread across his face. "It was

179

the other matter that I was reluctant to pursue. It is only by staying out of such matters and making no trouble that I have been allowed to stay in Williamsburg, being a Loyalist. Even though I know that you, Mr. Hutchinson, are the reason for my safety from the likes of Gates and his son, I still thought it best not to become involved. But if my daughter could be so brave and so determined to see the truth come out, I could not do otherwise."

Papa looked completely bewildered. "What did you do, my man? Please tell me!"

"I have known Carter Ludwell since we were boys in school," Robert Taylor said. "And I know how his mind works. He killed his own cows. I knew it at once. But my word means nothing at this point. The truth had to come from Carter Ludwell himself."

"Can you believe it, John?" Mama chirped. "He rode out to the Ludwell Plantation and convinced Mr. Ludwell to go to Clayton and drop these foolish charges before the magistrate came looking for *him*!"

"*Convinced* isn't quite the right word, Mother," Clayton said. "Mr. Ludwell was brought in practically by the scruff of his neck, and he looked as if he feared for his life."

"As well he should have," Robert Taylor said. "He was most eager to tell me how he set the traps—and then told your own servant that if he would witness to having seen your son Clayton set the traps, he himself would pay off the servant's indenture." He straightened his slender shoulders. "I assure you, sir, that is not what Loyalists stand for."

Thomas thought he heard Sam grunt in the corner. But for now, his eyes were on Caroline. She was glowing at him and he couldn't help but glow back.

Papa tucked his hands behind his back and stared down at his shoe buckles for a moment. When he looked up, his blue eyes were warm.

"Sir," he said to Mr. Taylor, "how can I ever repay you for your kindness?"

But Caroline's father held up his hand. "No repayment is necessary. Without your sense of justice, I would not have been here to come to your aid. As I see it, we are neither Loyalist nor Patriot. We are men."

"Men of God," John Hutchinson said. "Men are bound by God, not by politics. It is one thing to defend what you believe is best for people, and another to tread on the very rights you're fighting for."

Thomas held his breath. He was sure he had just seen something important happen.

"What of the Gates matter?" Papa said.

"Xavier Wormeley agreed to have their house searched," Robert Taylor said. His serious face brightened a little. "But I don't think he was happy about it."

Papa chuckled. "No one likes to have to admit he was wrong, eh?"

Just then a voice called out, "Mr. Hutchinson, sir!"

They all turned to the doorway where Esther had her head poked in. "The town crier's about, sir. I thought you'd want to know."

"That should be news about the war!" Sam cried. He came to life from his pouting corner and ran for the door.

"May I go and hear, Papa?" Thomas said.

"We must all go," Papa said. "I fear the news won't be good."

Everyone except Mama and Esther followed Sam down to

the Palace Green where a clump of people were knotted
together, waiting for the crier to pass. Caroline skipped to
keep up with them, but Thomas caught at her pink-flowered
dress and pulled her back.

"Well, Tom?" she said. Her face was smooth, but the
brown eyes had their telltale twinkle.

Thomas shrugged—and turned red. He looked down at
his shoes. "I just wanted to say . . . thank you."

"You're welcome," she said. "Do you want to meet at the
bridge tonight? I can't wait to hear all about the jail."

"You still want to be friends, after what I said about your
father?" Thomas said.

But Caroline didn't have a chance to answer, for the town
crier clanged his way past them, droning out from under his
wide-brimmed black hat in a voice that was even louder than
his bell.

"Hear ye, hear ye!" he cried. "General Benjamin Lincoln
and the Americans have been forced to surrender at Charleston,
South Carolina. Five thousand men are now prisoners of the
British. All Patriot leaders have been seized. All American
supplies have been taken by the British. Hear ye! Hear ye!"

"And Governor Jefferson refuses to rally Virginians to
fight!" Sam shouted after him. "Perhaps now he'll wake up,
eh?" He darted his eyes toward Robert Taylor. "And if he does,
there are some who should beware!"

He stomped off toward the college, taking off his tri-
cornered hat and beating it against his leg.

Thomas pulled his eyes from the vanishing figure of his
brother and watched the other faces that surrounded him.
They were all people he had come to know since he'd moved
to Williamsburg—Reverend Pendleton, Elizabeth Tarpley, the

red-whiskered leathersmith, Mr. and Mistress Wertherburn, and their slave girl, Cate. They were all looking very still, as if their lives had suddenly been changed.

Robert Taylor pulled his hat down on his forehead and quietly slipped out of the crowd, taking Caroline with him.

"Look there, Thomas," said his father beside him.

Thomas looked up in time to see a wagon creaking past with Peter Pelham driving in his black tri-cornered hat. In the back, glaring openly at the little crowd, were Henry Gates and his father, and sitting importantly beside them was Xavier Wormeley, jowls rocking with the wagon.

"It looks as if Xavier found just what Robert Taylor told him he would find in the Gates house," Papa said.

"Will they hang?" Thomas said.

"They'll probably just be run out of town when they're out of jail," Papa said.

Thomas nodded, but even the sight of Henry Gates being carted off couldn't keep his heart from breaking. Thomas was a Patriot and Caroline was a Loyalist . . . and now that was all that mattered.

As soon as Thomas had finished his chores the next day, he went to the apothecary shop for lessons. Alexander almost leaped over the counter to hug him and shake both of his hands.

"I knew something was going to happen yesterday," he said. "But I had no idea you'd end up a prisoner!" Alexander grinned and put his hands on his hips, just the way Caroline did. It sent a pang through Thomas.

"You know," Thomas said, "now that my father knows you're a Loyalist, he won't let you be my teacher anymore."

Alexander looked at him blankly. "What do you mean 'now that he knows'?"

"I had to tell him!" Thomas said. "I'm sorry!"

"Thomas!" There was a laugh hovering in Alexander's voice. "He knew I was a Loyalist the day he hired me. We talked about our politics right in his study."

Thomas felt his face scrunch up into a question mark. "But why did he take you on as my teacher?"

"Because I promised not to discuss the war with you, and he saw that you were learning from me. You are, you know." Alexander looked at him smugly. "So shall we begin the day's lessons?"

Thomas was too stunned to say anything. He only followed Alexander into the examination room. But when Alexander headed for the skeleton in the corner, Thomas jolted back to life.

"What are you doing?"

"It's all right, Thomas," Alexander said. "I asked Francis if we could use this bony fellow for a lesson, and he gave his permission. Francis is doing quite well, by the way. He should be back in here week after next, barking at you again—"

"But that's a . . . that's a skeleton!" Thomas cried.

Alexander grinned. "I see you've mastered that much."

"No! That's someone Francis . . . "

But the words died on Thomas's lips. Suddenly, it seemed stupid that he had ever thought Francis Pickering had killed his last apprentice and hung his bones in the corner of the examination room—just as it seemed ridiculous that he had ever thought the old man would hang body parts from the ceiling of the cellar. Or that Papa would hire a teacher he didn't know everything about. Or that Thomas had ever

refused to learn and had punched defenseless boys. Or that he thought he wanted to live anywhere but Williamsburg.

"Are you here, Thomas?" Alexander said.

Thomas nodded. "I'm here. Teach me about bones."

It was still light when Thomas passed the corner of Nicholson and North England Streets and hurried on to his house. He tried to push away the pang in his heart before it broke any more.

She won't want to play tonight—or any other night, he thought sadly. *I guess that's the way it is now*.

Thomas didn't know what to do with himself when he got home to the little house on the Palace Green. He was always out chasing imaginary villains with Caroline at this time of day.

Thomas wandered listlessly in the back door and was about to go upstairs to his room when he heard a voice in Papa's office. It said, very clearly, "Amen."

Papa had just finished praying. He was probably listening now. Something pulled Thomas toward his door. *I want to know what God's saying to him*, he thought.

The door was ajar, and Papa saw Thomas.

"Come in," he said. "I was just thinking about you."

Thomas settled himself on a green-checkered chair.

"Do you know what that meant today?" Papa asked. "When we heard the news about Charleston?"

Thomas shook his head.

"The capture of Charleston was the worst damage to the American cause since the war started," his father said. "Our army in the South now has no leaders, no supplies, and very few men to carry on. General Clinton can take all of South Carolina now with a butterfly net, and he won't stop there. There are North Carolina and Virginia still waiting to be ravaged by the King's army."

"There will be fighting here?" Thomas asked.

"There almost certainly will be. You'll begin to see the militia training on the Green right outside your window very soon, I suspect, and probably troops marching down from the north—British as well as Americans."

Thomas felt his eyes widen. "Will we be in danger here?"

"It's possible," Papa answered. "We must pray harder than ever." His face grew less square for a moment. "You understand how important it is to pray now, don't you, Thomas?"

Thomas nodded. "But you hate the war, Papa. And now it's coming right toward you."

"Ah, you are every bit as bright as Alexander claims, my son," Papa said. "Yes, I do hate the war. But there is no point in my resisting it anymore. It is here and it seems to be the only way we can win our freedom. That's what I wanted to tell you. I am going to begin to support the war effort—both here and on the Homestead and wherever else I have to go."

Thomas was sure his heart had suffered its final crack. "Will you go and fight?"

Papa put his hand on Thomas's shoulder. "No, son. I think I can be much more useful in other ways. But there are difficult days ahead. It's good to know I can count on you."

Thomas nodded solemnly.

"You can begin right now," Papa said. "I want you to do two things."

"Yes, sir."

"I have to make a trip to Newport, Rhode Island. I'm going to bring back plans for building warships. We will soon be building them on the Hutchinson docks in Yorktown."

Thomas nodded again, his head swimming.

"While I'm gone, you'll need to be the man of this house. You must take care of your mother and help Esther and Otis even more than you already have. You've proven that you're capable, have you not?"

"I hope so," Thomas said faintly.

Papa stood up from his chair and crossed to his desk. Thomas watched as he picked up the Hutchinson stone and smoothed his fingers across it. "Ever since I have been man of my house," he said, "I have turned to God before making every decision. At first it was hard to remember to do that, but this stone would remind me. Suppose you keep it for the same purpose."

Thomas stared as his father tucked the stone into his palm. It was as if he held a gold piece in his hand.

"Now then," Papa said, clearing this throat. "As for my other wish. I also believe that God puts people in our lives to help guide us, to hold us up when we want to give up. This Taylor girl—what's her name?"

Thomas hardly dared answer. "Caroline?"

"I think she is such a person in your life, Thomas. Be loyal to her as she is to you."

"But, sir," Thomas said. "She's a Loyalist!"

"Her father is a Loyalist," Papa corrected him. "She's 10 years old. She has yet to make up her mind." His father let a smile flash through his eyes. "Perhaps you can turn her around, eh?"

Thomas's smile sprang across his whole face as he wriggled in his seat, still clutching the stone.

"You can count on me, Papa—for both things."

"Then suppose you go see to the second. Right now," John Hutchinson said. His smile broadened. "I can see there's no keeping you in that chair."

The air was warm and velvety as Thomas flew across the Palace Green and tore around behind the abandoned Palace. Crickets were tuning up for an evening symphony and the first of the summer's fireflies were winking sleepily. But Thomas neither heard nor saw them. His only thought was that Caroline had to be at the bridge. She had to be.

He skirted the maze, stretching his neck like a crane to see. She would be waiting there, tapping her foot, ready to set Martha on him because he was late.

But his steps slowed to a disappointed walk. The bridge was empty. And so was his heart.

"It's certainly time you appeared, Tom Hutchinson," said a voice from above.

Thomas looked up to see a mass of petticoats and a pair of swinging feet. He tried to keep his voice from shaking as he answered. "I had business to attend to with my father."

"Good or bad?"

"Good," he said.

A grin as big as a slice of melon spread from one side of her mob cap to the other. "My father says we are going to need our loyal friends in the times that are coming. Is that what your father said?"

"Yes," Thomas said.

"Well, there you have it then, don't you?" she said.

"Come down," he said. "We have plans to make!"

As Caroline Taylor, his partner, climbed down from the tree, Thomas Hutchinson put his hand on his heart. It beat slowly and steadily. And it didn't hurt at all.

✟ ✟ ✟